DREAMS AND WISHES

Karren Radko

A KISMET® Romance

METEOR PUBLISHING CORPORATION
Bensalem, Pennsylvania

KISMET® is a registered trademark of Meteor Publishing Corporation

First Printing June 1993.

ISBN: 1-56597-070-5

Printed in the United States of America.

To my husband, Wayne Radko, without your support and encouragement, this book would not have been written.

To mom and dad, Jerie and Ev Kittell, thank you for the dream.

KARREN RADKO

Born in Arizona, Karren Radko has called many places home, thanks to her father's military career and a few additional moves since her marriage. "People associate me with the last place I lived," she says, adding, "At the moment, I'm thought of as a New Yorker." Karren resides in Oklahoma with her husband and two Samoyed dogs. She is passionate about writing and feels privileged to work at something she loves so much.

ONE

"He's good-looking, a real hunk, and rich, too," Ali proclaimed from behind the counter in the store. "And you're going to marry him."

Shaking her head, Skylar Carson strolled to the front of the small store and opened the outside door to a sunlit morning. "It was a dream, Ali," she told her sister, recalling the advice of the child psychologist in Tulsa. Reinforce reality, he'd instructed, but with care and love and humor.

"But it's not just a dream," Ali protested as she smacked a roll of coins against the cash register drawer.

Skye looked over her shoulder to see Ali counting out the money to verify the amount. Maybe her sister would forget about her dream by the time she completed the chore. Skye could hope, but doubted it. Once Ali got hold of an idea, there was no letting go.

The screen door squeaked when Skye stepped outside. She stood on the porch and peered up the sleepy street. Prospect, Oklahoma, once alive with humanity, was a dying town, and only a dog crossing the street broke the early morning tranquility.

She filled her lungs with the clean, sweet scents of early spring and listened to the wailing chirps of a scissortail as it called to its mate. Except for a crispness in the air, there was no hint of the rainstorm the night before.

Quiet as the morning was, Skye knew a handful of regular customers would soon come around. Thank goodness she'd converted her father's old office on the first floor of Carson Inn into a small store. Remodeling consisted of little more than adding a door to the outside and putting up shelving. Fortunately, a local carpenter whom her family had known for years had done the work cheaply. Of course, the expense of a refrigerated storage unit had been more than she'd cared to spend, but the income derived from the store paid for groceries and a few bills. Heaven knew, the inn wasn't bringing in an income amounting to much.

"Looks like it's going to be a nice day," Skye commented when she stepped inside. "I heard on the radio that some counties got hit pretty hard with high winds last night," she added in a effort to keep Ali's mind off her dream.

"Just some twisters." Ali closed the cash drawer. "Not any real tornadoes."

"That's true," Skye concurred. "No one was hurt, thank goodness, and the reports said very few of the twisters actually touched down. The ones that did were in outlying areas with no population."

"I know what you're doing," Ali said with a long face. "You think I'm silly to believe things like dreams, and you're trying to make me forget about it."

On the verge of denying the accusation, Skye thought better of it. "I've been caught," she admitted on a shrug. Pulling a large-toothed comb from under the counter, she stepped behind her sister and began threading it through Ali's long blond hair. "You need a trim. Why don't you head over to Mrs. Chamber's after school and let her cut an inch off the ends?"

"You're doing it again," Ali said in exasperation. "And I don't need a haircut yet."

"What am I doing?" Skye returned. "Besides brushing your hair so you'll be ready when your bus gets here."

"You know what I mean."

"Stand still," Skye insisted when Ali twisted and started to turn. "You've got a knot."

Ali obeyed but asked, "Don't you remember that time when Fluffy had her babies?"

"Of course I do."

"Then you remember that I knew the very night she was going to give birth 'cause I dreamt it."

"Yes, but—"

"Then there was the time I had that dream about getting my very own cassette player, and Mama got me one even though I never asked her to."

"Mama wrote me, told me about all the hints you dropped. It wasn't hard for her to figure out you'd like a cassette player for your birthday," Skye argued. "As for the cat, you knew she was going to have her babies any day. You were anxious and excited for them to come, and that's why you had that dream. Anyway," she added as an afterthought, "that was a long time ago. You were only six or seven."

"But I had the dream the very night Fluffy gave birth," Ali said adamantly. "And there was that time when you lost your car keys. You remember, it was a couple of years ago, right after you came home to stay. I told you where they were," she said proudly.

Arguing with Ali was futile, or so it seemed at times, and Skye silently admitted that she never could explain how Ali knew the keys had fallen out of her purse and landed under the bush beside the garage. "Okay, let's say some of your dreams are a kind of premonition," she offered to keep Ali from getting too worked up. "That doesn't mean they're all going to come true." The comb snagged, and Skye gently tugged at a knot of hair.

"Ouch."

"Sorry."

"This one will," Ali predicted.

"Well, maybe. But suppose it doesn't." As much as she fought the notion herself, Skye knew she and her sister could lose Carson Inn and the attached general store, but Ali refused to consider the possibility. The dream served as her escape from reality; at least that's what the experts had said about Ali's vivid imagination. They'd also told Skye not to worry, that with love and understanding, Ali was bound to leave her childhood fantasies behind. And for a while Skye had been optimistic that Ali was seeing things as they really were. Until recently, her sister's creativity had been channeled into oil painting. But the threat of losing the inn had brought on a new round of machinations.

"You know the money trouble we're having," Skye gently reminded.

"Sure, but we won't lose the inn," Ali replied cheerily. "You won't let it happen."

No, she wouldn't let it happen, not if there was anything she could do to save the inn. "Thanks for the vote of confidence, but I still think you ought—"

"Don't worry," Ali interrupted. "Even if you can't stop the bank from taking our place, he will," she said, emphasizing the *he*.

"Mmmm. *He* will," Skye mocked, paying no attention to the creaking of the front door, knowing old Mrs.

Garver, always the first customer every morning, had probably entered and was heading for the refrigerated section for her daily quart of milk to feed the dozen or more stray cats she'd befriended.

"Because he's rich," Skye added, recalling Ali's earlier characterization of the dream man.

"Mmmm."

"And kind."

"Very. And he's handsome and tall, over six feet," she continued dreamily. "And he's going to marry you, Skye."

Marriage was the last thing on Skye's mind, and Prospect the last place she would expect to meet a man fitting Ali's description. Skye tucked the comb back under the counter, then straightened to face Ali. "Let's see," she said thoughtfully. "He has light brown hair and a square jaw and, oh yes, bushy eyebrows. Isn't that what you said, Ali?"

"Not bushy," Ali corrected indignantly. "A little thick, but nice."

"Oh yes, now I remember."

"He's got the best eyes, all dreamy and kind, and they change all the time. Sometimes they're brown, sometimes green."

"Hazel," Skye told her, wondering why Ali was suddenly trying to stifle a giggle. "Ali?"

But all she got was more laughter, and she saw that Ali's gaze was fixed at a point behind her shoulder. She turned and, taking a step back, swallowed a startled scream before it became audible.

A tall man, over six foot, with light brown hair, thick, definitely not bushy, eyebrows, and hazel eyes stood in front of the counter grinning at her.

"He's here," Ali whispered in Skye's ear.

Mac Morgan stifled a chuckle, but he couldn't help

grinning, and after the hard night he'd had, the fact that he wanted to laugh at all was a surprise. The two ladies had been describing him, and the little one, Ali, claimed he was rich. A wild guess or wishful thinking, he figured, since at the moment he looked more like a pauper. He was supposed to fall in love and marry the older one, he gathered, and wondered which of the two ladies had seen him walking up the street and which one had decided to play a joke on him. He also wondered about their sense of humor.

Skye . . . that was the name of the woman, he recalled from overhearing her conversation with the girl. A pretty name for a gorgeous lady, he thought, admiring her long blond hair cascading halfway down her back, the elegant curve of hips clearly defined by the snug jeans she wore. And when she'd turned and faced him, he felt a tug in his chest as he found himself gazing into the bluest eyes he'd ever seen. She was tall, only a few inches shorter than his own six foot two, and he took her for twenty-seven, maybe twenty-eight.

Skye had to admit that the stranger's resemblance to Ali's dream man was uncanny. Spooky was more like it. One brow lifted, and his eyes twinkled with amusement.

He'd overheard their conversation.

Exactly how much, she couldn't guess, but certainly enough to prove embarrassing. Her cheeks tingled with a rush of heat, but she smiled back at him in an effort to regain her composure.

"Can I help you?" she asked, taking in the ragged look of him. His plaid shirt and jeans were soiled, and Skye noticed the missing button halfway down his broad chest. Stubble lined his square jaw, and he raked a dirty hand through unruly hair. He might look like

Ali's dream man, but he sure didn't possess the wealth of a Prince Charming. In fact, he looked every bit like a man in need of a handout.

"I thought so." He hesitated. "But now I think I'm supposed to . . . help *you*," he added, and gave Skye a wink.

Skye flinched, and something inside her fluttered at the seductive timbre of his voice. Next to her, Ali was starting to giggle. Although Skye wished she could shrink small enough to hide in a floor crack below her foot, she straightened, cleared her throat, and without averting his gaze, coolly said, "I don't need any help."

"That's not the way I heard it."

"You heard wrong," she said curtly.

"I don't think so," he persisted.

"Look," she said in exasperation, "I don't know how much of our conversation you overheard, but—"

"Enough to know you were talking about me," he interrupted, then leaned toward Skye and in a hushed tone asked, "Which one of you ladies saw me coming? You can tell me. What is it . . . some sort of a weird town ritual for greeting visitors?"

"Oh, we didn't see you at all," Ali piped in. "You were in my dream."

"A dream?" He was clearly confused.

Ali nodded, and Skye had had just about enough of this whole situation. "I'm sorry if you misunderstood," she began, but her apology sounded hollow. "I'm sure it must have seemed like we were talking about you, but I assure you that was not the case." She took in a deep breath. "Now, if you want to purchase something, then you've come to the right place, the only place in town, in fact, since Hawkins Grocery closed a few years back. If not, then perhaps you ought to be on your way."

"Whoa." Palms open, Mac lifted his hands in concession. The joke, or whatever it had been, was apparently over. "I sure could do with a cup of that coffee," he said, hunger in his gaze as he eyed the steaming pot.

"Help yourself." Skye watched him pour a cup, wishing he'd chosen to leave the store instead, but when he looked up at the sign listing the price, found herself saying, "It's on the house." She couldn't accept money from this man, not when he looked so needy, and although she'd been annoyed by his insinuations, couldn't blame him for misunderstanding the situation.

"No, it's not," Ali piped in, referring to the free coffee.

"Yes, it is," Skye corrected, and shot Ali a look that warned she should say no more. Fortunately, before Ali got a chance to speak, Skye heard the familiar rumble of the approaching school bus. "Time to go," she said.

Ali collected her books, but before heading for the door, she went to where the stranger stood sipping his coffee and thrust out her right hand. "I'm Ali Carson. I'm glad you're here."

"No more than me," he said on a smile, and returned her handshake. "I'm Mac Morgan."

"Ali." Skye's voice rang out from across the room. "You'd best be going or the bus will leave without you."

"Oh, all right," she conceded, and flashed a broad grin at Mac, then scampered through the door.

Sipping his coffee as he moved, Mac strolled over to the counter, where Skye had picked up a clipboard and was flipping papers. "This is great coffee," he raved, drawing her attention to him.

"Help yourself to another."

"It isn't really free?"

"Well, ummm . . ." She didn't want to make him feel like a charity case. She wouldn't do that to anyone. "Actually, it is. Providing free coffee to newcomers is a custom around here," she lied.

Mac smiled at her generosity. The free coffee was one thing, but the way she was trying to salvage his pride in the process touched his heart. "Where can I find a telephone?"

"Outside, around the corner."

He nodded and headed for the door.

"It's a pay phone," Skye blurted.

Mac spun to face her, and on a whim, scavenged deep in his pocket and brought out a couple of coins. He eyed them longingly, as though they were his last. "I think I've got enough."

Skye rounded the corner of the counter and walked toward him. There but for the grace of God, pricked her thoughts. "I've got a phone in the inn's lobby. You can use that one if you'd like." She motioned toward a closed door behind the counter.

"Thanks," he said, and followed her through it. His heels clicked on the polished wood floor when he entered the lobby. Wainscotting that shone as if it had been recently stained ran the length of the lower half of the walls; a delicate floral paper in pale blues and greens rose above, contrasting with the dark hue of the wood. A gold brocade settee angled from a corner of the room facing two wing-back chairs. His eye went to a blue and white checkered knit afghan draped over one of the chairs, then to a cabinet that overflowed with bric-a-brac. One entire wall of the lobby was decorated with framed photographs. From his angle, Mac couldn't make out any details of the pictures, but they were black-and-white and appeared old.

"Homey," he complimented.

"Thank you."

"You run this inn, too?"

"Yes."

"Between the inn and the store, you must have your hands full," he speculated.

"Not really. It's very quiet at the inn these days," she replied, thinking of all the empty rooms. They'd had one guest in the last three days, a fisherman who had checked out early this morning. "Anyway, the store's operating hours are limited to the mornings and Saturdays."

"No afternoon customers?" he asked.

"Everyone around here knows the hours, and should someone need something, they know where to find me. She led him behind a counter to an old rolltop desk, one that had the look of a genuine antique. "Phone's over here." Picking up the receiver, she handed it to him. "Help yourself."

Mac reached for the receiver, trapping her fingers under his grasp. "Thank you," he said, surprised, but pleased, that she didn't quickly pull away from him.

Skye gulped. The warmth of his touch spread through her like hot cocoa on a winter's night, and he was so close, she heard his steady breathing. She ought to be repulsed by his soiled, ragged clothing and unkempt appearance, but instead, felt herself being drawn to him. She lifted her gaze to see him staring at her. After an awkward moment, she removed her hand from beneath his and stepped back. "I'll be in the store," she mumbled, and left.

Mac watched the sway of Skye's rear end as she walked, and whistled low under his breath when she was out of earshot. The lady was potent, but he knew it was more than her good looks that attracted him. From their earlier encounter he knew she was spunky, and she possessed a generous nature. Beauty, spirit, and heart . . . lethal. With a shake of his head, he turned his attention to the telephone.

"Hello, Roger," Mac greeted when his assistant came on the line.

"Is that you, Mac?"

"The one and only."

"But how? Last I noticed, my cabin didn't have a phone."

"And it doesn't have much else these days, either."

"What are you talking about?" Roger asked, obviously confused.

"Your cabin got hit by a twister last night. It's in shambles."

"A twister. No kidding?"

"Believe me, it's no joke."

"But you're okay?"

"Yep. I'm fine." Mac proceeded to tell Roger how he'd been fishing last evening when the storm started. He'd been out of touch with weather reports, there being no radio, television, or even electricity in the cabin, so he hadn't a clue that the brewing storm would turn into more than a mild sprinkling of rain. "Weather turned ugly real quick," he said.

"Storms come up quick in that part of the country."

"By the time I picked my way through the woods and got back to the cabin, it was all over. I never even saw the funnel, but it left its mark." He told Roger how the swirling winds had rendered his jeep useless. The body was intact, but slumped on the rims of four flat tires, and Mac suspected the frame was badly damaged.

"As long as you're all right, the cabin can be rebuilt," Roger said. "Where are you calling from?"

"A small town called Prospect."

"Prospect," Roger repeated, then paused as though trying to place it in his mind. "Why, it's a good thirty, maybe forty miles from the cabin!" he exclaimed. "How'd you manage that?"

"Once I got to the highway, I hitchhiked. A farmer finally picked me up, and I couldn't be choosy about the destination."

"That town, if you can call it that, is no more than a dozen or two run-down stores and a string of old houses. There's nothing much in Prospect."

"Oh, I don't know about that," Mac said aloud, his thoughts drifting to Skye. "Prospect has got a certain something."

"I've no idea what that might be," Roger returned. "Want me to drive up and get you? I can be there in four hours."

"No, don't do that," Mac insisted. "At the moment all I want is a hot bath and a warm bed. I'm at the local inn and think I'll stay put until tomorrow morning. I'm sure I can rent a car in town or get a cab to take me to a place where I can."

Mac gave him Carson Inn's telephone number, Roger insistent that he wouldn't interrupt Mac's rest unless an emergency situation arose. "Shame your vacation is ruined," Roger said before hanging up.

Mac couldn't agree more. He hadn't taken time off in almost three years, not since his divorce. During that time he'd feverishly thrown himself into his work, doubling his already multimillion-dollar net worth. He'd gotten his start in oil during the boom of the late seventies, and he'd been smart enough to diversify in stock and land investment so that when oil prices fell, his overall financial portfolio was healthy. "The youngest millionaire in Texas," a Dallas newspaper had dubbed him. He was, after all, only thirty-five, but lately he'd been feeling much, much older.

He needed a rest, a change of pace. He'd driven himself for so long, at first to block out the pain of his failed marriage, later out of habit. In recent weeks, though, he'd been struck by the notion that his bank balance was growing by leaps and bounds, but the pleasure he was deriving from all that money was nonexistent. There was a world beyond the walls of his penthouse office and penthouse apartment, and he figured the first place he'd explore was Roger's backwoods cabin. Hunting, fishing, and simply wiling away the hours were to be his only priorities for better than a week.

When he went back to the store, Skye was ringing up a sale. A woman with silver hair and sloping shoulders paid for a quart of milk.

"Who have we got here?" the woman asked in a high-pitched voice when he entered.

"Mac Morgan, ma'am."

"Hmmm, Morgan." Her eyes drifted upward in a thoughtful pose. "Like the gas station," she said, making the connection to the Morgan stations that dotted the interstate.

"Like the gas stations, Elsie," Skye told the woman, then smiled at Mac as her gaze drifted up and down his length. "But not that Morgan."

"Oh my." Elsie eyed Mac but spoke to Skye. "Are you sure, dear? I mean, the name's the same."

Containing his laughter was difficult, but Mac managed to look halfway serious. Franchised to individuals, the pumps were filled with Morgan Enterprises fuel, but he couldn't admit that now. Not after the game he'd played with Skye over the cost of using a pay telephone, not when she was so certain he wasn't that Morgan.

"Morgan is a common name," he said with what he hoped was a straight face.

"I suppose so." On a disappointed sigh, Elsie Garver's shoulders dropped another inch or two.

Ali wasn't the only person in town to believe in the unbelievable, Skye thought as she handed Elsie the carton of milk. When the woman left, she turned her attention to Mac, who was eyeing the packaged donuts on a shelf. He had some change in his pocket, that much she'd seen for herself, but she doubted the coins were enough for the powdered sugar confections. She ought to turn away, ignore him until he left, but when his tongue hungrily glided over his lips, she could no more let him leave with an empty belly than she could let a dog die of starvation.

When he noticed her eyeing him, Mac strolled to the front of the counter. "Is there someplace to get breakfast?" he asked.

Was that his way of asking for a handout? she wondered. Then again, maybe he had a few bucks tucked away in one of his pockets or hidden in the sole of his boot. Her stepfather used to do that. "There's a fast-food place off the interstate."

He made a face. "Nothing else?"

"Not really."

"But isn't the interstate a distance from here?"

"Eight miles, give or take." He gave her a hopeless look. He didn't have a car, she guessed. That figured. In spite of his worn appearance, the whites of his eyes were clear, and she hadn't noticed the smell of alcohol on him. At least he wasn't a drunk.

"I can make you a meal," she offered, but quickly added, "Nothing fancy, just bacon and eggs." She was

rewarded with his smile, and once again experienced a
sensation of warm liquid filling every fiber of her being.

"Sounds good," he said.

Skye locked the front door and stuck a sign in the
window telling potential customers to go to the inn for
assistance.

"I appreciate this," Mac said, following her to the
inn, then down a hall leading to the kitchen.

"No problem," she said offhandedly, making light
of her good deed.

"I bet you're the kind that takes in stray animals,
too," Mac teased when she motioned him to sit at a
table in the center of the kitchen.

"Not me. That's Elsie's job."

"The woman with the milk."

Skye set a pan on the stove and turned on a burner.
"The milk she bought is for her homeless cats."

"What about homeless people? Where do they go
for help in Prospect?"

Her fingers trembled when she set strips of bacon in
the pan. What had she gotten herself into, and what
kind of handout was Mac Morgan looking for? Well,
whatever he wanted mattered little. Breakfast was what
she offered, no more. "We don't have homeless in
Prospect," she told him.

"None?" He sounded surprised.

"None that stay," she clarified. "There's no services
for them in town, but there is a homeless shelter over
in Lindsay."

"Is that a referral?"

Was that humor she'd heard in his tone? Surely not.
"I only mentioned it in case . . . in case you want to
know that sort of information." She watched the bacon
cook, careful to avoid his gaze, wishing she'd been a
bit more tactful.

"I am displaced at the moment," he muttered, "but I think I'll pass on the shelter."

The bacon sizzled when Skye turned the heat up, breaking the several minutes of awkward silence. She took a plate and flatware to the table and laid a place setting in front of him. "There's a bathroom down the hall if you'd like to wash up."

He took her up on her offer, and when he returned, his hands were a few shades lighter. Skye noticed that he wore no ring. She wondered what he would look like after a shave, shower, and in clean clothes. Her curious gaze met his.

"What?" he asked.

"I'm sorry. I didn't mean to stare."

"But you do want to say something to me," he supposed.

"You seem so . . ." Skye hesitated, and clicked her tongue against the roof of her mouth. "It's none of my business."

"Go on," he insisted.

"Well, it's just that you are obviously a very bright man, and I can't help wondering about . . . things."

Mac pressed his forearms flat against the tabletop and leaned his weight into them. "What things?"

"Do you do anything?" she asked in a small voice.

He chuckled. "I've been accused of doing lots of things." His laughter died and he shot her a flirtatious look. "What kind of *things* do you have in mind?"

Skye's embarrassment rose in her cheeks. Her question hadn't come out at all right. That's what she got for being nosy. "I meant what do you do to put food on the table?" she quickly explained. "I mean, do you have a skill or anything?"

His gaze glinted in amusement. "I'm a very skilled man."

Skye threw her hands up in resignation. He wasn't going to let her get out of this gracefully. Or maybe he simply didn't want to answer her question?

"My turn to apologize," he said a moment later. "You gave me coffee, a phone to use, and now breakfast. You're entitled to ask a few questions."

"I asked one, only one," she reminded him, and waited for an answer.

"Let's just say I do a little of this and a little of that."

She thought about that for a moment. "Like manual labor or fixing things?"

"You could say that." Indeed she could. He'd repaired more than a few financially ruined companies. "Yep, that's what I do."

"Then you move around a lot?" Skye speculated out loud, already guessing at the answer to that one.

Move a lot? Mac had to think about that a moment. He stroked the scratchy patch of hair growth circling his jaw. Actually, he'd been in Dallas for years, and he figured business trips didn't qualify as moving from place to place. "Sure, I get around a bit," he ended up saying for lack of coming up with anything better, then wondered at Skye's disapproving expression. Nothing he'd told her could have come as a surprise. She had obviously pegged him for a drifter from the first moment they met. And why not? Hell, he looked worn as a secondhand pair of boots, and admittedly, he'd done his bit to confirm her assumptions.

He ought to stop the game playing and tell her who he really was. He should, but didn't want to. Skye was the first person in years to treat him like a regular human being, and it felt great. When she spoke, it was to Mac Morgan, not his money. And the generosity she'd shown him hadn't been inspired by the size of his bank account. Besides, what harm was there in his little game? He wasn't hurting anyone, and he wouldn't be around long enough for Skye or anyone else to know any better.

Still, accepting handouts wasn't in his nature. Especially not from a woman who, from all appearances, barely eked out a living. What kind of income could be earned in such a sleepy little town? Not a big one, he silently answered his own question.

"I'd like to pay for the meal," he said.

"I didn't ask for money," she reminded him.

"No, but I want to."

Skye poured coffee into his cup, and felt guilty that she'd misjudged him by fearing one breakfast would turn into a month of free meals. His unexpected pride was a pleasant surprise. "Very well," she said. "Pay me whatever you think appropriate."

"I'll do that," he murmured, and gave her a smile that would melt snow in winter.

TWO

"Thanks, Rudy," Skye said to her customer when he handed over the price of a loaf of bread and a pound of butter. The old-timer had called her to the store, leaving Mac alone in her kitchen.

Her suspicious side warned that she was crazy to leave him, a stranger, alone. Yet intuitively she trusted him. She shook her head against the irrational thought. For all she knew, he was a thief and had used the opportunity to rummage through things. She pictured the cashbox she'd inadvertently left in plain sight in the lobby earlier this morning. There wasn't much money in it, but she would sorely feel the loss of even a few dollars.

"When you gonna get some chewing tobacco in this place?" Rudy asked, but Skye knew it wasn't a serious request.

"Now, you know you don't chew anymore," Skye returned playfully. "Why, if I carried that stuff, you'd be tempted to pick up on bad habits again, and you've got enough of them as it is."

Rudy chuckled and looked pleased. "Right about that."

She handed him his purchases. "Now, shoo, you old fool," she said lovingly, earning his wide grin, which exposed two missing front teeth. "I've better things to do than argue with you all day."

"Heh, heh," he clucked, and headed for the door. "I'm a-goin', but I'll be back."

Soon as Rudy was gone, Skye scurried next door, stopping at the counter in the lobby to examine the contents of the cashbox. She let out the breath she'd been holding. All the money was there. As she tucked the box in its customary locked drawer, she fought a twinge of guilt by reminding herself that she knew nothing about the man she'd taken in and fed.

Back in the kitchen, she found Mac sitting contentedly at the table, drinking his coffee. He shot her a broad grin when she entered.

He stretched and patted his stomach. "Great meal," he raved. "Thanks."

"I'm glad you liked it," she said, and started collecting the dirty dishes from the table.

He stood and followed her to the sink, catching her wrist when she went to run the water. "Let me clean up. It's the least I can do."

Midmorning sun streamed through the window over the sink and played in Mac's eyes. Emerald flecks sparkled and danced in a sea of golden brown, and she was lost in their depths. For a moment she forgot to breathe, but then managed a deep intake of air and broke away from the pull of his gaze.

"Thanks for the offer," she said, her voice sounding tinny, even to herself. "But you don't have to do this."

"I want to," he insisted at the very moment the bell in the lobby jangled, announcing someone was looking for assistance, probably in the store. Skye excused herself and searched out her customer.

Mac found the dish soap in the cupboard under the sink, and minutes later, eyed the dishes he'd washed, which now lined the drainboard. He yawned, a reminder of his sleepless night. There was a bit of coffee left in the automatic brewer, so he lifted a clean cup and poured himself some.

Leaning against the counter, he inspected his surroundings. The kitchen, like the inn itself, was old-fashioned, the four walls lined with ancient white appliances and scarred wood cabinets, leaving a large, square open area in the center for the table. A black and white tiled linoleum floor showed years of wear. In spite of its age, the room was spotless and uncluttered.

The hot coffee stung his tongue when he took a taste. Blowing across the rim of the cup to cool it off, he wondered about Skye Carson. What possessed such a beautiful young woman to stay in a place like Prospect, tied to a business that was obviously going downhill? And he wondered if she was always so trusting, taking in total strangers as she'd done with him. He might have been anybody, might have wanted to steal from her, or worse, he speculated, anger at her naïveté welling up inside him at the ugly possibilities. She needed someone to take care of her. She needed a man, she needed . . . He gulped as though attempting to swallow the thought that came to him so easily. She needed him. That's what he was thinking. He shifted uneasily, trying to throw off the notion. He'd been working too hard, been cooped up in that office of his too long. That's why his thinking was muddled. After all, he'd only just met Skye Carson. By a quirk of fate, they'd come together, and by this time tomorrow, she'd be no more than a memory. Then why did his gut ache at that thought?

Minutes later, when Skye finished in the store, she found Mac occupying a chair in the lobby. His legs outstretched and crossed at the ankles, he was in a half-sitting, half-lying position. His head slanted against one shoulder and his eyelids were closed. She approached him slowly, trying to decide whether or not she should disturb him. After all, a customer could enter and be put off by a raggedly dressed man napping in the lobby. But when she neared to within a couple of feet, his lids fluttered open, causing her to take a step back.

"Sorry, guess I nodded off," he said, his voice husky with fatigue.

"Evidently."

He stood and stretched, then pulled a few dollar bills from his pocket. "For breakfast," he explained, holding them up to her.

Skye eyed the singles in his hand. She didn't want to take them. For all she knew, the three dollars was the last of Mac Morgan's money.

"Isn't it enough?" he asked.

"More than adequate," Skye quickly answered. "Too much, in fact."

"Three dollars doesn't seem like much for a home-cooked meal." Once again he held the money out to her.

Skye accepted the bills and headed for the counter behind her. "Tell you what," she said as she took the cashbox from the drawer. "We'll split the difference." She counted out the change and handed him a dollar fifty. "I can't take that much money for a few eggs and a couple of strips of bacon."

"What about the buttered biscuits, juice, and coffee?

Bet it doesn't cover the cost of them." But seeing her determined look, he took the change and stuffed it into his pocket. "Thanks."

"You're welcome."

"You've gone to a lot of trouble for a stranger, and I appreciate your generosity, particularly since I got you running back and forth between here and your store."

"It wasn't a problem," she told him sincerely.

"I hope not."

She'd fed him and provided a brief respite from the outside world. He would leave now, and Skye found herself more than a little curious about a man as attractive as he, and intelligent. Why would such a man choose the life of a roving handyman? She wanted to ask, but didn't. He was entitled to his privacy, and whatever his circumstances, none of it was any of her business. Besides, she doubted she'd ever see him again, and the less she knew about him, the better. As it was, something about him touched her too deeply for comfort.

"Well, Mr. Mac Morgan." Skye held out her hand to him. "Nice to have met you," she said pleasantly.

He took her hand, but instead of shaking it as she'd expected, held it in place. "You think I'm leaving," he stated.

"Of course, I assumed . . ."

"I'm not."

Good grief! His thumb lazily stroked her hand, and concentrating on anything but the waves of heat that pulsed up her arm was impossible. "You're not?"

"No. I need a room for the night."

"But . . ." But what? What was she thinking? Oh yes, now she remembered. Was he able to pay her for a room, or was this to be charity?

As though he'd read her thoughts, he said, "I can pay," then sheepishly added, "If it's not too much."

Carson Inn, the largest structure in Prospect, hovered sleepily at the edge of town, several hundred feet from its nearest neighbor. Raw land lay to the south. Sloping, treed hills, thick underbrush, and a lake that was distant but visible from the inn were all on Carson Inn property. The weathered, old inn housed a dozen guest rooms of various sizes, all on the second floor. Skye and Ali's private quarters, Mac had learned, were on the first floor. His room, one of the smallest, was at the end of the long hall that ran the length of the upstairs.

He was certain the rate Skye quoted him was no more than half the amount of the normal cost, but he was too tired to bicker over the price, and had a feeling she'd stubbornly stick by her quote, no matter what.

He took in the rectangular space of his room. Simply decorated, the room was furnished with a bureau, an overstuffed chair in a corner, and a bed. One wall was papered in blue and white stripes, the others painted white. The bedspread and curtains were a solid blue, and like the rest of the inn, the floors were hardwood.

"This is fine," he told Skye, who hovered in the open door clutching the partially filled bucket of water she'd plucked from the hallway floor outside his door. The roof leaked when it rained, she'd told him, quick to add that his room was free from any such annoyances.

"Bath's over there." She motioned toward a closed door. "It's shared with the room next door, but the inn's empty, so you'll have complete privacy."

"Long as it has running hot water, I'll be happy."

"Of course it does," she said sharply.

He'd hurt her feelings. "Sorry. All I meant was how much I want a shower."

Her scowl abated. "Of course. I'm a bit defensive where the inn is concerned, I suppose."

"It's okay."

She moved into the hall but turned back toward him before leaving. "If you'll set your clothes outside the door, I'll wash them."

Mac looked down at his soiled shirt and jeans. He was in no position to argue. "Thanks," he said, but she was already walking away.

He went to close the door, discovering the latch refused to catch. Upon closer inspection, he found that the door had shifted, only a little, but enough to create a mismatch with the catch and the opening in the frame.

There was a time when he'd been pretty good with his hands. After he rested, he would see what he could do to effect a repair. For the moment, he closed the door, overconfident it would stay put unless someone deliberately pushed at it. With no other guests staying at the inn, that wasn't likely to happen. Satisfied, he stripped out of his clothing and headed for the shower.

Fifteen minutes later, wrapped in a towel, he set his dirty garments outside the door, then dropped onto the bed, and on a big yawn, fell asleep.

Downstairs in the lobby, Skye closed the inn's reservation book and, with a thud, set it on the desk. Two visitors scheduled in the next three weeks were the only entries. Of course, there were bound to be a few people who would stop in without reservations: warm-weather vacationers who took the scenic route instead of the interstate, a fisherman or two who would come to test their luck with the bass in the lake.

At least they'd be fully paying customers. Head tilted, she looked in the direction of Mac's room on floor above. And bound to be less troubling than her current guest.

Pushing back in her chair, she remembered a time when she was a little girl, a time when her father and grandfather were still alive. Those were carefree days. Everyone was happy then, and the inn was always full of guests. Would it ever be like that again? When she came home to Prospect two years ago, she'd been certain she could rejuvenate the place. Now foreclosure seemed inevitable.

"Skye Carson, stop all this doom and gloom," she ordered herself. For several seconds she practiced smiling, a technique she'd learned a few years ago at a self-improvement seminar in St. Louis that the company she worked for had sponsored. She used the method to make herself feel better whenever she was low. The learned skill was the single remnant from her life in the city, and maybe the one good thing to come out of her five years there. No, that wasn't true. Only the last year had been bad. But why was she thinking about all that now? Because until Mac had walked through her door, she hadn't been attracted to a man since then.

Skye cleared her mind of unwanted thoughts. After several forced smiles, she began to feel better, downright silly, in fact, even giggled over what people might think if anyone saw her sitting there wildly grinning like a madwoman.

Prepared to tackle anything, she left her office. With a jaunt in her step and a smile on her lips, she proceeded upstairs. First stop, the guest room occupied the night before. In record time she scrubbed the bath, vacuumed, dusted, and stripped down the bed.

Next stop, Mac's room. From down the hall she spotted his clothing piled up outside his door, and when she neared, bent to pick up the articles. Her hip brushed the handle as she straightened, causing the door to open several inches.

Surprised, Skye backed off and stared at the handle. She heard Mac's heavy, rhythmic breathing coming from the room. Guessing he must be sleeping, she stepped forward and reached for the handle, intending to close the door.

If only her gaze hadn't drifted into the room, to the bed. When she saw him, she froze, her hand stuck to the knob as if it had been glued in place, and her pulse raced at an alarming rate. Mac was facedown on the bed, and except for a corner of a towel flanking one side of his waist, he was naked.

His head faced the window, so she couldn't see his features, only a tumble of light brown hair that was damp from shampooing. One arm was under the pillow, the other dangled over the edge of the bed. Her gaze drifted down the slope of his hairless back and rested at his narrow waist.

Skye's lower lip quivered. She should leave, but her legs refused to move. In spite of the shabbiness of his clothes, she'd known he had a good physique, but looking at him now, she'd been unprepared for the unabashed beauty of Mac Morgan.

His skin glistened from a recent bath, and she inhaled a lingering scent of soap that smelled as heavenly as the lilac bush in bloom in her garden. Hesitantly, but irrepressibly, her gaze slid a bit lower, following the firm mounds of his buttocks. Her breathing grew ragged as her eyes traced a pattern down his muscled thighs, grazing in the mesh of fine hair covering his legs.

And then he moved. Without warning, Mac flipped onto his back. Startled by the suddenness of his action, and even more by the unencumbered view of his sex, all rigid and pink, and oh so big, she gasped. All at once the clothes dropped from her hands; she scurried to pick them up, hitting her head against the doorknob when she rose. Reflexively she groaned from the unexpected impact.

"Having trouble?"

She glanced up to see Mac leaning on one elbow, staring at her through heavily lidded eyes. He'd stretched the towel across his maleness.

"No—uh—n-no trouble," she stuttered. "I was picking up— I mean, getting your clothes and—"

"And having a little look," he accused.

That did it. As embarrassed as she was, and she sure couldn't remember a time when she'd been more so, she hadn't deliberately spied on him. "How dare you," she said, full of venom. "I'm no Peeping Tom, and besides, you're the one who left the door open."

"But I didn't invite you inside," he returned.

"And I sure wouldn't have come in if you had," she said furiously. "All I did was come to pick up your clothes. Anyway, you haven't got anything I haven't seen before."

"Then why are you so hot and bothered?"

His amused grin annoyed Skye more than his question. "I'm not," she said in a huff.

"In that case, you won't mind if I get up?" In a single movement he began to rise and reach to pull the towel away, but didn't manage it before she fled the room, leaving Mac with a smile as wide as the Oklahoma horizon.

He'd been dreaming about Skye when she woke him, and had felt a stab of embarrassment, not so much because of his nakedness but because she'd been the cause of his erection. Thank goodness the lady couldn't read minds or he'd be in big trouble.

He lifted his wrist to check the time, then remembered he'd lost his Rolex in the twister. A digital clock on the dresser confirmed what his heavy eyes told him. He'd slept no more than two hours. Ragged as he felt, he doubted he'd get back to sleep, not after the way Skye had woken him. The muscles in his stomach were still knotted from the shock of opening his eyes and seeing the real flesh-and-blood woman in his room. For an instant he'd believed he was still dreaming and almost jumped out of bed to grab her and bring her down under him.

"Hmmm, you should have done that, ol' buddy," he said with regret, and speculated about Skye's reaction. Wrapping the sheet turban style around his body, he stretched out on the bed, dwelling on his missed opportunity, and fell back to sleep minutes later.

Meanwhile, still hot with indignation, Skye hovered over the washing machine in the basement. "How dare you, Mac Morgan," she reprimanded, and eyed his clothes lying on the floor beside her. The scrappy jeans and shirt were to blame. At least the fact that he hadn't been in them was the problem. Instead of cleaning his things, she wanted to rip them to shreds, but fought the urge. Mac had no other clothing, and she didn't need a naked man running around the inn, something she didn't put past him.

The image of him in the altogether temporarily defused her anger. Visualizing his taut body, his maleness, she shuddered. He was gorgeous.

Stop this! she commanded. There was no denying Mac's attractiveness, but she'd blown his good looks all out of proportion because her love life hadn't exactly been exciting in the last couple of years. Prospect wasn't overflowing with young, eligible men, and she could count the number of dates she'd had on one hand and still have a couple of fingers left over.

Mac's arrogance rankled her. He'd practically accused her of voyeurism. Skye punched the knob on the washing machine, and the tub filled with water. While she added the soap, her glance fell on a bottle of liquid starch. With a wicked gleam in her eye, she snatched it from a low shelf and gave the tub water not one but three healthy doses of the liquid.

When Jim Lennox, one of Skye's long-standing customers, stopped by for a few purchases from the store, she asked him to take Mac's cleaned and folded clothes upstairs and drop them off by his door. She'd also included shaving cream and a razor that she'd taken from the store. Jim gave her a quizzical look, but did as she asked without question. Skye wasn't going to risk a second run-in with an insolent, naked Mac Morgan.

She stood behind the counter in the lobby when she heard Mac's booted footsteps on the stairs. Tensing, she hoped he wouldn't bring up the subject of their earlier encounter. She wanted to forget the whole thing. Keeping her gaze focused on the inventory logbook in her hands, she sensed when he came to stand in front of her on the other side of the counter, but didn't look up until he spoke.

"Thanks for the clean clothes," he said, but made a face and rubbed at an irritation at his neck, then added, "I think."

Skye kept a straight face. "Something wrong?"

"No," he answered quickly, but scratched his skin under the stiff shirt and shook a leg as though trying to throw something off.

She'd starched his underwear, too, and figured it was taking all his restraint to keep from scratching himself in places that wouldn't be considered polite in public.

"About earlier," he began tentatively.

Oh no! "Forget it," she said with a wave of her hand, and felt an instant rush of heat in her cheeks.

"I can't do that."

"Well, I can," she fiercely replied, and gave her attention back to the book she held in the hope that he would stop talking about her inadvertent invasion of his—she gulped, a wave of remembered images flitting uninvited into her thoughts—privacy.

Could she really forget so easily? Mac had noticed, not to mention thoroughly enjoyed, her lusty expression when he'd caught her in his room. She had wanted him. He couldn't have mistaken that look.

"I just wanted to apologize," he finally offered.

Skye looked up from her book. "Oh?"

"I know you didn't barge in on purpose."

"I didn't barge in at all," she corrected.

"Yes, well . . ." He stuck his hands in his pockets, and Skye noticed his jaw working. "However you came to be in my room," he continued, emphasizing the *however*, "I know it was an accident and I shouldn't have given you a bad time."

"Accident?" Skye harped.

He shrugged. "Sure."

"I don't think that word applies." Her voice rose as she spoke. "I think you deliberately left your door open. I think you're a flasher."

Stunned by her accusations, Mac stood dumbfounded for several seconds. But as he watched her lips purse together in a pout and her blue eyes shoot daggers at him, all he could think about was how delicious Skye looked when she was angry. He shot her a wicked grin. "Following that line of thinking, I suppose I deliberately shrugged the covering and the towel off my body in my sleep?"

"Probably." Skye straightened and crossed her arms

in front of her in a challenging stance. The developing scenario was bordering on the ridiculous, she knew, but she couldn't back off now. Why couldn't Mac have simply said he was sorry instead of qualifying his apology? "I bet you heard me coming and only pretended to be sleeping."

He laughed outright at that, a deep, throaty sound that vibrated through the lobby, but settled down enough to add, "I'm a smart one. Even made sure I had no other clothes to wear."

"It's not funny," she declared, but he didn't stop laughing.

Mac swiped at his watering eyes. He didn't think he'd ever laughed so hard in his life, and it felt great. "Maybe you ought to call the police," he got out between choppy breaths. "Have me arrested as a pervert."

"I might do that," she said with a seriousness that she wasn't feeling. His laughter, combined with the absurdity of their argument, was wearing on her. She glanced up at him again, but immediately looked away and made a futile attempt to stifle her own laughter. The next moment she abandoned all restraint, and before she knew what was happening, they were both hysterical with laughter. When one of them would almost stop, the other would say something and they'd start up all over again.

"Police, I'll call them," Skye repeated between chortles, breaking them up all over again.

"Pervert," Mac blurted, adding to their merriment.

He'd stepped behind the counter, and Skye found herself no more than two or three inches from him. Although tapering off, they were still laughing when his hand came down on her shoulder and he gave her a tender squeeze.

"I am sorry about before," he said, starting to turn serious.

Skye's lashes lowered. "Me, too."

"My lock is broken," he suddenly said.

"What?" Confused, she looked up at him.

"The lock in the door in my room. It doesn't latch. That's why it wouldn't stay shut."

Comprehension came into her features. "I bumped into the door when I collected your clothes, and then you were . . ."

Mac waited for her to finish, but she just gave him a pleading look. He was tempted to remind her that she'd lingered a foot or two inside the room, but didn't want to risk her ire again. Instead he said, "I understand."

But Skye didn't. She could have turned and left the moment she discovered Mac on the bed. Ashamed she hadn't done that very thing and feeling guilty over the invasion of his privacy, she'd retaliated against him instead of facing the fact that she wanted to look at him.

"Skye?"

"You're right about one thing," she said tentatively.

His hand cupped her chin and lifted until she was forced to meet his gaze. "Tell me."

His fingers against her skin felt like hot embers, and his eyes, more brown than green in the long shadows of afternoon, bored into her as he waited for her response. "When I saw you in your room," she started hesitantly, "I could have left right then, but I didn't."

His smile was easy and somehow comforting. "Why?"

"Because I wanted to look at you," she admitted. "I'm sorry. I took advantage."

"Yep."

"I can't take it back," she said, assuming he must be annoyed with her.

"Nope."

"You're angry."

He shook his head and chuckled. "Of course I'm not."

"I would be if the circumstances were reversed," she pointed out.

"I'll have to remember that," he told her, his tone so serious that Skye stepped back, out of his reach, and her heart skipped a beat. The image of Mac seeing her nude, examining every angle of her body as she'd done his, flashed in her mind, and the temperature in the room suddenly shot up several degrees.

Mac wanted to kiss Skye. Actually, he yearned for lots more, but would settle for a taste of her lips. In one fluid movement, embracing the hope that she wouldn't pull away from him, he narrowed the space between them, and took her in his arms.

His lips were coming down on hers when Skye heard an unexpected sound and jerked away from him. Ali, a dreamy look on her face, stood in the doorway sighing.

"Go on and kiss," she enthusiastically ordered. "Don't mind me."

"Ali!" Skye pushed away from Mac.

"It's only a kiss," Ali exclaimed. "And I want to watch."

Skye cleared her throat and took a couple of seconds to regain her composure. "There's nothing to see."

"No kiss?"

"No."

"Darn." Ali studied Mac as she walked toward him. "You clean up good."

"I'm glad you approve."

"How was school?" Skye asked, drawing her sister's attention. When Ali turned in her direction, Mac excused himself, saying he was going for a walk, leaving the two of them alone.

"So how was your test?" Skye referred to a geography quiz Ali had been studying for.

"I passed. That's all that matters."

Ali wasn't studious and never missed an opportunity to knock academic studies. On the other hand, she loved all art forms, excelling in anything creative. Skye accepted her sister's artistic bent, even admired it, but knew that Ali needed a diploma if she was to do anything with her life.

"You can't get into art college without a high school diploma," Skye reminded.

"But I'm only in the eighth grade," Ali objected. "I'll make better marks next year."

"It's only going to get harder," Skye persisted. She had promised their mother to do her very best by Ali, and even if she sounded like a shrew sometimes, her sister's education was important. "I'm sorry to push you." Skye patted Ali's arm. "I'm concerned, that's all."

Ali's hard look softened. "I know, and I'll try harder."

Skye stretched one arm over Ali's shoulder. "I know you will."

Ali scrunched her nose, a gesture Skye was all too familiar with. Something was coming, and she prepared herself for whatever Ali was on the verge of saying.

"You like Mac," she stated.

"I don't dislike him," Skye carefully said.

"But you like him?"

"I suppose." Skye shrugged. "He's okay."

"Are you kidding? He's a hunk."

"Even so, looks aren't everything."

"But he's nice, too."

"Ali." Skye faced her sister head-on. "We don't know anything about him. He's a stranger and he'll leave in the morning."

Ali's expression shifted to surprise as she mulled over Skye's words. Then she looked into Skye's eyes and, in a level tone, said, "He's not leaving tomorrow. He can't. You haven't fallen in love with him yet."

THREE

"What the heck?" Skye pressed her palms against her ears to muffle the sharp sounds that resembled rapid hammering. She looked up. The noises were coming from the second floor. Before she could investigate, the telephone rang.

"Carson Inn," she answered, and flinched from a new sound: high-pitched drilling.

"I understand you run a nice clean place," a woman's voice said. "A quiet place."

"Yes, quiet," Skye got in just as another round of thudding started up. She covered the receiver with her hand, but it wasn't in time. Then, thankfully, the sounds stopped.

"Are you sure it's a quiet place?"

"Oh yes," Skye assured. "Are you calling for reservations?" Please, no more hammering, she silently begged.

The woman, Mrs. Benson, and her husband were visiting a relative in Prospect and needed a place to stay, a quiet place where Mr. Benson's high blood pressure wouldn't be triggered.

"We came directly to my sister's house," Mrs. Benson explained. "Goodness, I haven't seen her in years, and she's had a passel of kids since. My poor husband simply can't take all that noise and scampering about. Not to mention, my poor sister already has her hands full without having to look after us, too."

"Who is your sister?" Skye asked.

"Anne Richardson. She referred me to your establishment. My husband and I would like to check in this evening." Skye heard some new noises, this time coming from Mrs. Benson's end and sounding very much like children at raucous play. "Right away if that's possible." The woman's voice quavered.

"No problem," Skye confirmed as a new round of pounding coming from the upstairs started again.

"What is that noise?" Mrs. Benson wanted to know.

"Nothing to worry about," Skye hoped. "Believe me, it'll stop in a minute and you won't be bothered."

The woman accepted Skye's assurance and reserved her best and most expensive suite for two nights. After entering the name in the reservation book, Skye headed for the second floor. Wearing a stern frown, she took the stairs two at a time and spotted Mac and Ali at the end of the hall in front of Mac's room.

"Oops," Ali warned Mac when Skye approached. "Here comes a grouch. We're in trouble."

"What are you doing?" Skye asked, looking back and forth between them.

"Mac is fixing the door," Ali answered. "And it's almost done."

Of course, the door. Skye's temper subsided, especially since no harm had been done by all the racket. She'd booked the couple. "You didn't have to do that," she told Mac.

He gave her a quick glance, his attention immediately

drawn back to the door he balanced in place with his hands. "Yes, I did," he said, the corners of his mouth arching in a taunting grin. "If I want privacy, that is."

"I was planning on giving you another room," she countered.

"I like this one." He glanced her way, his eyelids at half-mast. "Memories and all that."

Skye ignored the allusion to their earlier encounter. With Ali present, what else could she do?

"Your sister showed me where you keep the tools. Hope you don't mind that I helped myself."

"Not at all."

"Ali," Mac said. "Can you steady this door while I bolt it to the frame?"

"Sure thing." She stepped up to the door, but then shifted gear and moved back. "You better let my sister do it. I have to study now."

"Study? Now?" Skye repeated.

"You said you wanted me to do better in school," Ali reminded.

"Yes, but you volunteering to study is a twist."

Ali started walking down the hall. "Only doing what you want," she said over her shoulder.

Behind Skye, Mac cleared his throat, drawing her attention. "I'm still waiting for an assist," he said when she looked his way.

"Oh, of course."

Skye held the door upright as Mac screwed in the upper bolts, then bent to take care of the lower ones. "I hope my sister wasn't making too much of a pest of herself."

"She's a remarkable girl," he said, glancing in her direction. From his hunkered position, his gaze fell on her crotch, and seemed to stay there an eternity before traveling upward.

Nervously Skye moved away from the door. "I don't need to hold it anymore," she said in explanation.

He gave her a suspicious look but took the weight of the door against his shoulder and went right back to the task at hand. "She's got quite an imagination," he continued. "Ali's been telling me about all these—" he paused, searching for the right words, "—expectations she has."

"Her dream," Skye said with dread.

"Mmmm."

"I'm sorry you had to hear all that."

"Don't be. It explained so much more about the conversation I overheard between you two this morning."

At this point that was a relief, Skye thought. Now he knew for sure that she hadn't been making fun of him or flirting with him, or any other thing he might have imagined.

"Ali completely believes in her fantasies or dreams or whatever she calls these premonitions of hers," he commented. "She cited several instances when she'd successfully foretold the future."

"Ali sometimes twists the truth," Skye explained. "She doesn't lie; at least she doesn't mean to. I think she simply doesn't want to see the reality of situations." She thought about her sister's belief that they wouldn't lose Carson Inn. "Sometimes it worries me," she added.

"Have any of her premonitions come true?" Mac asked, thinking he wouldn't mind if there was some merit in Ali's prediction about a relationship between himself and Skye. Of course, that wasn't about to happen since he was leaving in the morning.

Skye pondered his question, a difficult one to answer. There'd been a time or two when Ali's predictions had been fulfilled, fueling her fantasies even more. She relayed the story about her lost keys.

"Could be your sister has a gift."

"You don't actually believe in all that hocus-pocus?" Skye asked, full of chagrin.

Mac inspected the bolts he'd tightened, then stood and faced Skye. "I'd like to," he said, his tone husky, and seeing the surprise in her eyes, added, "But you don't?"

"No," she said with certainty. "Almost everything Ali's predicted can be attributed to reasoning and common sense."

Mac took a couple of steps toward Skye until he stood directly in front of her. "And those things that can't be explained?"

"I'm sure there's some sort of logical answer," she said stubbornly, her chin jutting out. "Even if it's not readily evident."

His gaze locked on to hers in a way that made Skye's throat go dry. "You're quite the pragmatist, Skylar Carson."

He stood so close, she had to crook her neck to look at him. "If believing in those things I can see and hear makes me pragmatic, then I plead guilty."

"But what about dreams?" His hand reached for a straying lock of hair that curled down her cheek, his fingers brushing her skin before setting the golden strand behind her ear. Her cheeks warmed and tingled. "Don't you have them?"

Skye gulped, the dryness in her throat growing as Mac's penetrating stare intensified. "I have dreams," she managed. "I hope and plan for things as much as anyone."

"Ah, but you can't imagine the impossible coming true," he stated, his tone lowering to a husky drawl.

"In heaven, yes. On earth, no," she answered with a tight voice. "Down here, what we see is what we get."

Mac inched closer to her by the second, and as though an unseen hand guided her movement, she felt herself steadily pulled toward him. His mouth drew up on one side in a provocative grin, and his eyes fired emerald sparks. He looked tantalizing. Even the stubble outlining his jaw, thicker and darker than this morning, possessed a strong appeal, and she wondered at the feel of it against her skin.

He crooked a brow. "There's such a thing as perception, and everyone's is different," he said with gentle authority. "And sometimes things and people aren't at all what they appear to be."

Word games. Skye wasn't interested in playing, but she knew one thing: She was attracted to this man in a way she'd never experienced, and knowing that he wouldn't be around in the morning did nothing to abate the magnetic effect he had on her. When his lips inched toward hers, all she could think about was Mac's mouth on hers, his arms holding her close.

For the second or two that his mouth hovered just above hers, Skye trembled in anticipation. Then he kissed her, gently at first, his lips exploring hers, sending sparks up and down her spine. Then his mouth came down hard, and she moaned her desire and stepped into the circle of his arms. The stubble lining his jaw bristled against the tender skin framing her lips.

His hands explored her back as his tongue mapped the softness of her mouth. She returned his kisses, her body burning with passion until she thought she was on fire. Bringing her hands up, she combed her fingers through his hair, loving the clean, soft feel of the short tendrils. Her other hand ventured down his arm, and she reveled in the tautness of skin and muscle.

When Mac pulled away, she felt as though all the breath had been sucked from her, and she temporarily wobbled on weak legs. He smiled at her tenderly, and she knew how easily she could slide into his arms, anytime, anyplace. But he was leaving in the morning, she remembered, and stiffened against a sudden thud in her chest and stepped back.

"I'm sorry," Mac apologized. "I shouldn't have done that."

"You didn't do anything I didn't want," Skye admitted without looking directly at him, hoping he wouldn't notice how much he'd affected her. "Anyway, it was only a kiss," she added, but didn't believe it for one minute, at least not as far as she was concerned.

Mac, on the other hand, had probably held many women in his arms. She was simply another diversion in a continuous round of new people and places. Like Henry Walker, her stepfather, he was one of those men who always needed to know what was over the next hill, and nothing, not money, family, responsibility, or even a woman, could keep him in one place very long.

"You're going to wear *that*?" Ali pointed at the royal blue halter-style dress stretched across Skye's bed.

"We have guests staying with us," Skye answered matter-of-factly, then returned her attention to her reflection in the mirror. She ran her fingers through her hair, letting the curls fall back to her shoulders. She would leave it down, she decided, and reached for a tube of lipstick.

"So what?" Ali flopped onto the bed and leaned her weight into one elbow. Curiosity registered in her voice. "You don't usually put on a dress unless . . ." Through the mirror Skye saw her sister's eyes widen and mouth slant into a knowing grin. "Unless you want to impress somebody."

Skye picked up the blue silk from the bed. "I want to look nice, that's all," she insisted, pulling the dress over her head.

"Mac will like it," Ali said confidently when Skye stepped into matching blue slings.

"I'm not dressing for Mac," Skye insisted with more conviction than she felt. She'd told herself she wanted to look festive in the hope she would begin to feel that way, too. The closer the bank came to foreclosure on the inn, the harder it was for her to maintain a positive outlook, and she needed something to raise her spirits. But beneath all the rationalization, she hoped for Mac's approval, but certainly couldn't admit as much to Ali.

"He's nice," Ali said dreamily. "Don't you think so?"

"Who?"

"Mac, of course."

"He's okay," Skye agreed with a casualness she didn't feel, all the while picturing his muscled body stretched out on the bed, remembering the feel of his mouth and his arms.

"He's more than okay," Ali persisted. "I can tell you like him, and he likes you, too—lots."

Skye sat at the edge of the bed and let her hand glide over her sister's crown of gold curls. "I do like him, Ali. He was nice enough to repair the door, but we don't really know him, do we?"

"I do," Ali insisted petulantly.

"No, Ali, you don't."

"But I saw him in my dream."

Ali was impossible at times, especially when her premonitions were challenged. Once again, Skye found herself wishing she hadn't missed so many growing years of her sister's life. But between their age difference and the years she had spent away at college, then the years in St. Louis, Ali had been little more than a stranger when Skye returned home. Too often she felt inept at handling a thirteen-year-old, especially one with such a vivid imagination.

"Let's say you did visualize Mac in a dream," Skye said with resignation in her voice. "He's not exactly how you pictured him," she pointed out.

"No," she answered softly, but in the very next moment, bounced to a sitting position and, her enthusiasm back, said, "but I know you two are going to be together. Everything is going to work out."

Skye knew Ali's *everything* referred to the inn. "You have to realize we might not be able to hang on to this place," Skye told her as gently as she could. "I've tried everything I can think of to keep the inn, but, Ali, it isn't working." She hated the distress she heard in her own voice. "I'm not saying it's hopeless," she added. "We have an option or two, but you, both of us," she corrected, "need to be prepared in case the worst happens."

Ali abruptly stood. "But this is our home, and you promised Mama that you'd look after it."

Skye felt a stab at her heart recalling the promise she'd made her mother on her deathbed. She'd promised to do everything within her power to keep the inn, and swore she would take care of Ali. Neither had been easy, and at the moment Skye felt as though she were failing at both.

"I am trying, Ali."

Her sister turned, then wrapped her arms around Skye's neck in a sweet embrace. "I know you are, but you don't understand." She stepped back and looked up at Skye. "Everything will work out. You'll see."

The time had come to try a different approach. Skye had to find some way to jar Ali's belief in her fantasies, otherwise she might never accept the inn's loss, if it ever came to that. "Didn't you tell me the man in your dreams was rich?" she asked.

"You know I did," Ali confirmed on a shrug.

"Mac Morgan is a poor man, a drifter, a man who can't stay in one place long enough to put down roots. And he definitely isn't the sort to dedicate himself to earning a fortune." No matter how softly she tried to say it, her words sounded harsh even to herself, but Ali had to accept the facts. "You know I'm right," she added, after an awkward silence. "He's a lot like Henry," she said, her tone more hushed than before.

Ali scrunched up her nose at the comparison. She had liked their stepfather, maybe even loved him since she was a mere eight years old when he married their mother. But she'd also been very hurt when he walked out of her life, leaving her to wonder what terrible thing she'd done to make him leave. After six months of professional counseling sessions and numerous talks with Skye, she came to understand that she wasn't to blame. But she had suffered so many losses for a child—first their father, then Henry's sudden departure, then their mother's death. Now her home was being threatened. Was it any wonder she clung to unrealistic hopes? Skye thought. Nevertheless, Ali had to see Mac for who he was, and that definitely was not some hero come to save the day. Otherwise she was likely to be hurt again.

"Don't expect too much from Mac," Skye warned. "You'll be disappointed."

"He's not like that," Ali proclaimed. "I can't explain why he isn't exactly like I pictured, but I know he's kind and nice and won't hurt you or me.''

"He's leaving tomorrow," Skye reminded in exasperation. "So it doesn't much matter what either of us thinks about him.''

"Humph." Ali spun on her heels and headed for the door, but before leaving, glanced over her shoulder at Skye and with a knowing smile, winked. "We'll just have to see about that,'' she said, and there was no denying the challenge in her tone.

Mac loped down the stairs, a whistle on his breath, laughter in his heart, and a growl in his stomach when he inhaled the hearty scents of Skye's home-cooked dinner.

He hadn't felt so good in a long time. Clean country air combined with a leisurely day when his biggest decision had been which drill bit to select for repairing the door had something to do with his mood. But Skye had much more to do with his deep-down good feeling.

He smiled thinking about her. Never had a kiss been sweeter and more thrilling all at once. He accepted that in large part his exaggerated response to the charms of Skye Carson were due to his self-inflicted hermit lifestyle of the last few years. Work and more work had been his living motto, one that had greatly enhanced his fortune but left little time for a social life.

There had been women, but their numbers were few, and his relationships with them had been limited to attending social functions where a lady on his arm proved an asset. He'd accompanied one or two home on occasion, staying on until dawn, but never with anyone who made more out of a one-nighter than he did. He made no promises, and his response to their charms lasted no longer than the momentary urges of his body.

He never let them inside to see the man under the Armani suits and money clip brimming with big bills. But in Prospect, he was Mac Morgan, a drifter, claiming no more than the clothes on his back. Maybe that's why Skye had rocked him with no more than a kiss, freely given; he didn't have to wonder about her ulterior motives. Something he could never say about his ex-wife.

A genius at turning a dollar, or so business associates claimed, he'd entirely missed the mark when it came to unraveling the mysteries of his wife. Why he couldn't see she had married his money, not him, bewildered him to this day. She had seemed so sweet, so genuinely supportive and caring, that it had taken two years of her constant unfaithfulness before he began speculating about her true nature.

Mac drifted into the kitchen and spotted Skye stirring a pot on the stove. His heart rate picked up at the sight of her long, shapely legs sticking out from beneath the short hem of a dress, her thick, shiny hair curling lazily about her shoulders, and the creamy skin bared halfway down her back.

"Delicious," he declared, and she turned in his direction.

"You haven't tasted it yet!" she exclaimed.

He referred to Skye, not her dinner, but he said, "No, but I'm definitely anxious to."

She chuckled, and he loved the throaty sound of her laughter. "You look beautiful," he said from the doorway, almost afraid to step closer since he wasn't at all sure he could refrain from pulling her into his arms.

"Thank you." She sounded pleased, but her attention didn't leave the stove top.

"Can I help?" he asked, and risked a few steps inside.

"You bet." She motioned toward a stack of plates on a counter. "You can take those into the dining room and set five places."

"Five?"

"We have other guests," she explained. "They're upstairs but ought to be down any time."

Mac passed directly behind Skye in order to collect the dishes, and inhaled the sultry scent of her perfume. He wasn't so hungry anymore, not for food anyhow, but he sure could devour her.

As if she'd read his thoughts, she glanced in his direction, sending him a smile that was as seductive as any he'd seen. And her eyes. He didn't know eyes could be that blue. The hue of her dress complemented them perfectly, bringing out their full color.

"The plates," she reminded.

Mac stiffened and headed for the counter. "I'm supposed to set the table."

"You offered," she said with a gleam in her eye and a glow on her cheeks.

He gathered the dishes. "Any special seating arrangements?" he asked on his way out.

"Any way you want," she assured him, and he reluctantly made his way into the dining room, where every second away from Skye seemed like forever.

Minutes later the dining room filled with more people, three to be precise, than Mac wanted. He pictured Skye across an intimate candlelit table set for two, not at a sprawling table where she worried that everyone's water glass stay filled and their plates full.

Ellen and Ralph Benson introduced themselves and sat across from him. Ali sat to his right, and when Skye came to the table carrying a large platter of succulent roast beef, Mac rose and helped her center the dish on the table.

"Allow me." He stepped behind her chair and settled her into it.

"We're from Des Moines." Ralph addressed Mac once he was seated. "The wife and I are here visiting her sister. Where are you from, Mac?"

"Here and there," Mac answered indecisively. "I move around." He glanced at Skye and thought he noticed a quick look of disapproval cut across her features, but then she was smiling again.

"Is that so?" Ralph continued. "Are you a salesman?"

"No." Mac fidgeted in his chair, uncomfortable with the man's questions. "I . . . umm . . . do odd jobs."

"He fixes things," Ali chimed in. "Mac repaired one of our doors today," she told them with obvious pride.

"Isn't that interesting," Ellen piped in, the disapproving look on her face belying the sweetness in her high-pitched midwestern twang.

"What line are you in, Ralph?" Mac asked in an effort to draw the conversation away from him. The ploy worked. From that moment on, talk around the table centered around the Bensons, their farm, and their family.

"Great meal," Mac told Skye, taking a second slice of her homemade bread. "You're quite a cook."

"Thank you."

"So was Mama," Ali said, her tone carrying a hint of sadness.

Mac wanted to ask about the woman who had mothered Skye and Ali. He knew so little about the Carson girls, he realized, but something in Skye's expression, a hint of sadness, he thought, when Ali had mentioned their mother, warned that he shouldn't ask questions.

At the end of the meal Ralph leaned back in his chair and addressed Skye. "I didn't want to bring this up during dinner," he began, "but there's a leak in our bathroom, and the wife and I are hoping you can do something about it."

"Drip, drip, drip," Ellen mimicked the sounds. "We won't be able to sleep tonight with that faucet going."

"I'm sorry for the problem," Skye apologized. "There is a man in town who knows his way around plumbing. Unfortunately, I heard he's suffering from flu, and doubt I'll be able to get him out here right away."

"Oh dear," Ellen anguished.

"Mac can fix it," Ali offered.

"I can move you to another room," Skye told them, apparently not hearing, or ignoring, Ali's suggestion. "The suite across the hall is similar to the one you're staying in," she continued, adding, "The sitting room is much smaller, but, of course, so are the charges."

"Move again?" Ellen complained. "Why, we only unpacked before dinner."

"Mac can fix it," Ali repeated, this time louder, then looked up at him. "Can't you?"

"Well, I . . . a . . ."

"You can," she insisted.

"Probably," he agreed. "If it's something simple, and you have whatever tools I might need."

Skye's frown showed her disapproval. "We can't ask Mac to repair a leak," she told Ali sternly.

"We have lots of tools," Ali told Mac, ignoring Skye.

"We'd appreciate your having a look," Ellen pleaded sweetly.

Mac leaned back in his chair. "No promises," he said. "But I'll look at it."

Everyone smiled approvingly, except Skye. Her

brows knit together, she said, "It isn't right to ask you to do this."

"I'm happy to," he returned, and meant it. Before she could argue further, Mac rose and spoke to Ali. "Come on, little one. I'll need my helper."

Ali glowed at his suggestion and obediently followed him upstairs. Once on the second floor, she took the lead and showed him into the Bensons' room.

"I hear it," he announced, opening the door to the adjoining bath.

"Drip, drip, drip," Ali mocked Ellen. "Like she said."

The sounds came from the sink, and after a brief inspection, Mac assured Ali that he could indeed make the repair, providing he could get his hands on a new washer.

"There's lots of stuff in the shed." Ali reminded him of his previous visit to the work shed, a large outbuilding full of all sorts of tools and supplies.

She followed him outside and turned on the light when they entered the dank enclosure. Dust hung in layers over everything.

"Amazing," Mac muttered, and began scavenging shelves for pliers and washers.

"What is?" Ali wanted to know.

"All this stuff, just sitting here, and no one uses it."

"Skye isn't good about fixing things. I'm not either."

"Why do you and your sister stay here?" he ventured, eyeing shelf after shelf of clutter.

"It's our home," she said, as though that explained everything.

"Then you two have always lived here?"

"Not Skye. She left for a long time, but came back

a couple of years ago." Her gaze shifted from him to the floor. "Right before Mama died," she added.

Mac set a reassuring hand on Ali's shoulder. He wouldn't ask her more questions, not if the answers were painful. When she glanced up at him, he smiled down at her, thinking how much she resembled her older sister. He'd bet he was seeing Skye at that age. "Let's find what we need and get out of here," he told her, "before we start hacking from all this dust." His feigned cough accentuated his statement. Ali giggled and followed him down another aisle of tall shelves.

Minutes later, after finding what he thought was the exact size washer he needed, and pliers, they headed for the inn.

"I'm glad you're here, Mac," Ali told him, and in the soft light of dusk, took his hand and led him along the darkened path to the back door. "Skye needs a man," she suddenly blurted. "She doesn't think so, but she does."

Mac didn't know how to respond, but Ali touched him deep in his heart. He wasn't sure about Skye needing a man. She might not be able to make repairs to the inn, but he'd seen enough of the lady to guess at the streak of independence she possessed. Mac suspected Ali was the one in need of a man in her life, someone to love as a father. Some part of him wished he could be that man.

Thirty minutes later, he straightened and eyed the sink. "Success," he announced after several dripless seconds had ticked by.

"I knew you could do it," Ali praised from behind him. "This old place has so many things that need fixing," she added on a sigh. "If only you didn't have to leave in the morning."

Mac turned to face Ali, whose wistful look made him wonder what she was thinking. He knew she wanted him to stay, and figured she was hatching some plan to get him to do that very thing. He ought to be thinking about rebuttals to anything she might come up with, but to his surprise, he didn't want to find reasons to leave. He wanted to stay. Hell, he'd planned a week and a half off, and by his count, that left him with seven or eight days.

"I'd like to hire you," Ali said with a seriousness beyond her years.

Mac didn't dare laugh. "Thank you for the offer, but how will big sister feel about it?"

"I own the inn, too," she gushed. "It's as much mine as Skye's. Just because my portion is in trust until I'm of age doesn't mean I can't make decisions."

"No, of course not," Mac was quick to agree. "Usually partners talk to each other before making decisions, though."

"This is different," she insisted. "We need someone to make repairs. Skye can't argue that."

As if she possessed some telepathic powers herself, Skye picked that very moment to enter. Arms crossed in front of her, she stood behind Ali.

"And how do we pay Mac for his labors?" she asked, making a startled Ali spin around.

"We'll find a way," she stuttered.

Skye looked beyond Ali to Mac. "I'm sorry for putting you in the middle of this," she began. "We do have lots of things around here that need repair." She paused and drew in a deep breath. "We simply can't afford to hire on a handyman right now."

Mac sensed how much it took for Skye to admit that she couldn't pay him. "I'm cheap," he offered on a whim.

She shook her head. "We can't pay anything."

"Not even room and board?"

She looked at him in amazement. "You'd work for so little?"

"For a few days," he assured her, but when she looked skeptical, added, "And I've got a few bucks stashed away to tide me over."

In your boot, no doubt, she was on the verge of saying, but caught the words before they slipped out.

"Have I got the job?"

Ali, like Mac, looked to Skye and waited for her decision.

Skye was trapped and in trouble no matter how she answered. To say yes would give credence to Ali's dream, but a no would make her look mean-spirited. And logically, she couldn't find cause to turn down his offer.

"We could use a good handyman," she conceded, and for Ali's benefit was quick to add, "but only for a few days."

Mac relaxed, aware for the first time just how tense he'd become while awaiting her answer.

FOUR

Skye rose at her customary early hour the next morning, showered, donned a pair of jeans and knit top, piled her hair on top of her head, then made her way downstairs, where she prepared breakfast for her guests.

The Bensons were up and ready to be served by seven and out the door by eight, telling Skye not to expect them until dinner. After cleaning up after the morning meal, she straightened their room and made the bed with clean sheets, then went to check on Ali, who manned the store.

Three customers stood in line at the register when she entered via the inn's door. Saturdays were always busy, but even if every day brought the same business to the store that Saturdays did, profits wouldn't be enough, not by a mile, to put a dent in the staggering bills she'd inherited along with the inn.

She joined Ali behind the counter and gave the last customer, a farmer from several miles down the road, a warm smile and a wave of her hand as he headed out of the store.

"Lots of sales this morning," Ali said cheerfully, closing the cash drawer.

"Saturdays are always good," Skye said. "Maybe you bring the place luck," she teased.

"I could stay home from school and bring it luck every day," Ali offered.

"I don't think so."

"At least I've got two whole days when I won't have to look at a history book or think about higher mathematics." She scrunched up her nose. "Like algebra."

"One of these days you're going to wish you'd been more serious about school," Skye warned.

"Not me. An artist doesn't need math."

"But she does need a diploma."

"I guess," Ali conceded with difficulty.

A few more customers strolled into the store over the next hour. Skye drifted in and out to help Ali if needed, and in between, dusted and polished the inn's downstairs living areas and lobby. All the while her thoughts drifted to the second floor. Mac still wasn't up when she finished and went back into the store.

"Looks like we've hired a late sleeper," she complained to Ali.

"Mac?"

"Do we have other employees?"

Ali harrumphed. Her eyes narrowed, and she shot Skye a triumphant glance. "He's not in bed."

"Mac didn't come down for breakfast," Skye pointed out. "In fact, I haven't seen him at all."

"That's because he got up earlier than you," Ali said smugly. "I saw him when I went to the kitchen for a glass of water."

"Then where is he?" Skye wanted to know, wondering if she'd provided room and board to a man who intended to give nothing in return. Mac might be more like Henry Walker than she'd guessed. Certainly Henry took advantage of every opportunity to sponge off people, and he made plenty of promises he never meant to keep.

"He went out to the shed," Ali said.

Skye verified the midmorning hour on the wall clock. What on earth was Mac doing in the shed this whole time? If he was there at all. "We'll see about that," she said, more to herself than to Ali.

Minutes later Skye followed the rock path that cut a walkway through the backyard. A cluster of redbud trees marked a section of the path, their dense blooms creating a palette of delicate pinks. Approaching the shed, she noticed two side windows had been opened, and heard movement coming from inside.

The door stood wide open and a gust of dusty air assaulted her nose when she entered. Skye sneezed, and Mac suddenly appeared and gazed at her from behind a tall, fully stacked shelf.

He strode toward her, wiping dusty hands at the sides of his pant legs as he moved. "Mornin', boss lady." Mac beamed. His hair was tousled, and dust bunnies clung to the edge of one brow. Once again Skye was struck by his handsome good looks that oozed masculinity. Although the day was too young to be hot, Skye felt warm and dabbed at the dampness forming at the base of her neck.

"Did you come to check on the new employee?"

"Of course not," Skye said a little too quickly, and felt a new wave of heat rushing her. This time its cause was pure embarrassment. Surely he couldn't read minds. "I came out for the mower, and I want to check on the supply of fertilizer," she rattled on. "I think we may have enough left over from last year to cover the grass." The lawn was in need of its first trim of the season, so she wasn't actually fibbing.

"I piled the bags over there." Mac pointed to a far corner.

Skye spotted the neat stack, then surveyed the rest of the work shed, noticing the dust-free countertops, the shelves neatly stacked with storage boxes, and the tool area, where each drill, saw, and hammer occupied its own space on a shelf or hanging from pegs on the wall. And everything looked oiled and cleaned.

"You did all this?" she asked in amazement.

"Can't do a job unless you have the right tool, and you've got to be able to find it first."

She glanced over at Mac, who stood a few feet away. Morning sun streamed through the open window. Gold hues played through his rumpled hair. She couldn't resist a lazy scan down his lean, muscled length. His stance was pure male. He stood facing her, legs and back straight, booted feet planted inches apart from each other. She worked her way back up his body, stopping a moment at the glistening patch of skin peeking through the unbuttoned top of his shirt. When she reached his eyes and realized he, too, was doing an inspection . . . of her, Skye's pulse jumped and she stepped back awkwardly.

Mac doubted he could ever get tired of looking at Skye. And the things she did to his body were unbelievable. Every time she was in the room, his stomach fluttered as though an invasion of thousands of little creatures had commenced, and his whole body pulsed in desire. He'd seen women dressed in outfits that cost thousands of dollars, their bodies adorned with magnificent jewels, but he could think of no woman so appealing as Skye. Her well-worn jeans fit snugly, hugging her rounded hips, and a white knit top stretched over the fullness of her high breasts. Her thick hair was piled high on her head, held in place by a thick elastic band, and sparkled in the morning sun. Several strands had escaped their confinement and roamed at will around her forehead and down her cheeks.

She wore no makeup, he noticed. She didn't need any. Skye was perfection. He especially liked the way her cheeks tinted when she was embarrassed or excited, and at the moment, as his gaze continued a slow inspection of her, they were a rosy pink. He hadn't deliberately tried to make her feel uncomfortable, but hell, when she stood a few feet away, teasing every fiber of his being with her charms, how was he to keep from ogling her?

"Fair is fair," he proclaimed. "Don't expect me to apologize for staring."

"What?" she asked in surprise.

"You got a mighty good look at me yesterday, and I figured I owed you one." He winked, and from her startled reaction, knew he'd made her more uncomfortable by referring to the incident in his room the day before. "Of course—" he paused and thoughtfully touched his forehead "—maybe not so fair after all, since you have clothes on."

"Aren't you ever going to let me forget about that?" she asked, so seriously that Mac flinched.

"Hey, I was only teasing."

"Well, stop," she returned harshly.

Mac came to attention and saluted. "Yes, ma'am. You're the boss." She was definitely sensitive about the topic. After the kiss they'd shared, he hadn't thought she would be. Remembering the warm, wet feel of her mouth, he longed to repeat that particular experience, but given her mood, decided against any move on her, for the moment anyway.

She eyed him critically for several seconds, and he thought another reprimand was coming, but then he saw the tension in her body ease and she again surveyed the room.

"This looks great," she praised, apparently willing to change the subject.

"Just doing my job."

"Yes, but I appreciate the effort. This place needed a good cleaning. Every time I came out here, I'd think about doing it myself, but it was such a big project and there was always something else that needed doing." She sighed and let her fingers glide across a cutting table. "Then, too, I'm not very good with mechanical things."

Mac thought about what Ali had told him about Skye's not being handy and, although Prospect was her home, the fact that she'd only returned two years ago. "Ali told me you'd been away for years," he ventured. "And I can guess that whatever you did for a living, it had little to do with a hammer and nails."

That earned her smile. "That's for sure."

Mac asked, "What made you come back here?"

Her mouth tightened. Evidently Skye disliked his question, but she said, "I didn't have much choice." In the next instant she moved to the far corner of the room and counted the bags of lawn fertilizer.

"There should be enough for one pass," she speculated when Mac stepped beside her.

"I'll get started on it right away," he offered.

"Yes, I suppose you might as well do it," she thought out loud. "It'll give me a chance to catch up on some paperwork."

"I noticed the back porch has some loose slats, and a few others are rotting."

"There's some lumber in here somewhere," Skye

said. "If it's usable, I suppose you might try to make some repairs."

"I found the lumber, and it is in good shape. So is the saw," he said, and when she gave him a skeptical glance, added, "I tried it earlier. A little oiling and it worked well enough. The only thing I'll need is paint."

"I saw some cans of the same color that's on the porch," Skye offered.

Mac shook his head. "It's old and thick."

"Then we'll have to get some more, but there's no place in Prospect to purchase it. There's a store in Lindsay, though."

"No hurry. It'll be a couple of days before I get around to painting, but I will need enough to do the entire porch. What's on there now is faded and will never match a fresh coat."

"All right," Skye agreed, but Mac sensed her hesitation and wondered if she worried over the cost of paint or the painter himself.

Skye entered the inn, and after checking the telephone answering machine in the lobby, which she'd switched on, she went to the kitchen. She had closed the store briefly in the afternoon, leaving a note of explanation on the outside door, to drive Ali into Lindsay where she was watching the Saturday matinee with Mary Lipcot, her best friend.

She collected a bowl of cooled boiled potatoes from the refrigerator. Potato salad ought to go nicely with the ribs she intended barbecuing on the grill. Standing in front of the kitchen sink, she began peeling the skins away, her gaze drifting out the window in the direction of the erratic humming sounds of the lawn mower in action.

Mac's back came immediately into view as he moved

up the lawn, making long row patterns in the grass. He wore no shirt. A tremor wound its way through Skye in response to seeing his bare skin glistening from perspiration in the sunlight, his muscled arms taut and working as he pushed the machine. Surprisingly, his skin was fair as though it had witnessed little sun. The light shade seemed at odds with his rough features and fit form. Of course, the gray, cold days of winter were still a recent memory and could account for his lack of color, she supposed. It's just that any "handyman" she'd ever encountered had sported sun-drenched skin. But she thought no more about it when Mac came to the end of a row, spun the mower around, and, seeing her through the window, sent her a smile and a wave of his hand.

A minute later Skye headed through the back door, a tall glass of ice water in hand. Mac saw her coming and pulled the mower's throttle down. The machine sputtered to a stop.

She offered him the glass. "Thought you could use this."

He swiped his damp brow with his forearm, then took the water. "Thanks." He drank it down in huge gulps.

"Sorry about this old machine," Skye said, studying the rusting mower in an effort to get her thoughts off his chest, off the firmness of his flat stomach, off her impulse to touch him. "It's seen better days."

"The motor cut out a few times," Mac informed her. "I made some adjustments to the gas intake and cleaned the blades. She's been running pretty good since."

Skye listened as he spoke, but her gaze never left the mower or the lawn. "It's a large yard," she commented. "Did you have enough fertilizer?"

He stepped alongside her, causing her to shift nervously from one foot to the other. Her skin dampened, and she knew she wasn't reacting to the unusually warm day.

"It was enough," he said. "I laid it down thin, but you've got healthy grass here, so it ought to be fine."

"It's all the rain we had this year. Made it grow faster and greener than ever before."

From the patterns in the lawn, Skye judged he'd cut better than half the yard. "Did you have lunch?"

"No. You weren't around, and I didn't want to rummage through your kitchen."

Skye risked a side glance at him and immediately felt a jab somewhere deep inside. Stripped to the waist, Mac was potent, and she couldn't help recalling the vision of his exquisite naked body in bed. She wondered what kind of a lover he would make, and instantly scolded herself for the thought.

Awkwardly she turned and headed for the kitchen door. "I'll make you a sandwich," she said in her retreat.

"Give me a holler when it's done," he called to her, then she heard the mower's motor rumble to a start.

Ten minutes later she waved to him from the back door and sighed in relief when he collected his shirt from the porch railing and put it on. But he didn't bother with the buttons, and Skye's gaze immediately drifted down the line of bare skin when he entered.

"Ummm, looks good," Mac said enthusiastically when she set a plate with two sandwiches on the table in front of him.

"It's roast beef left over from dinner last night."

He took a huge first bite, and in no time at all, one of the thick sandwiches was gone. He hadn't had breakfast, she recalled. "I've got some carrot cake," she said en route to the refrigerator. After cutting a large piece for Mac, she sliced a smaller one for herself.

When she sat across the table from him, she saw he'd put a major dent in the second sandwich.

"That's a lot of lawn you've got back there," he said between bites. "I hate to think about you mowing it by yourself."

"I manage," she said, with deliberate irritation in her tone. She wasn't helpless, and she and Ali had done quite nicely before Mac Morgan showed up on her doorstep.

His eyes met hers. "I've no doubt about that," he returned, calming her annoyance. "This cake's wonderful," he complimented after testing a bite. "Did you make it?"

"Yes, it was my mother's recipe. I may not have inherited my father's skills with repairs, but, like my mother, I can cook."

"Indeed you can," he said, the timbre of his tone deep and simmering.

He finished the cake quickly, and Skye cut him another piece. He was a big man, with an equally large appetite made bigger from skipping meals and engaging in physical labor. She took pleasure in the hearty way he ate everything she put in front of him.

She had doubted Mac's enthusiasm for hard work, but her opinion was rapidly changing. After witnessing the miracle he'd performed in the work shed, after which, without a break, he'd moved on to the lawn, she began to think she'd struck quite a bargain.

But how long would it last? she wondered. At any time Mac was likely to decide he'd had enough of lawns and paints and hammers . . . and her, and move on to another town.

So what if he did? she asked herself in the next breath. Mac wasn't a part of her life. He was only someone passing through it, and if he wanted to stick around a few days, exchange work for room and board, then that was fine with her. Of course, there were bound to be financial costs involved with the repairs he would make. Purchasing paint was probably only the first unexpected and unbudgeted expense. If she lost the inn, the repairs and money spent would be for naught. But she mustn't think that way. She'd told Ali they still had possibilities to explore, and she'd meant that. What she hadn't said was that actually there was but one chance to turn the tide of financial ruin. Carson Inn's future was in the hands of her father's old friend, Milo Craft.

"Where did you live before you came back to Prospect?" Mac asked, drawing her attention to him.

"St. Louis," Skye answered simply. She hesitated to tell him too much about herself, as though talk of personal things would somehow bring Mac into her life, and, of course, that was not going to happen. Yet she couldn't deny how attracted she was to him, and in spite of all the very real and very sound reasons she shouldn't get close to him, she found herself yearning to open up to him, to tell him things she'd spoken about to no one.

"St. Louis is a far cry from Prospect," Mac observed.

She nodded in agreement. "It took me quite a while to get used to such a big city. Just when I thought nothing could shake me anymore, I went on a business trip to New York."

"Now, there's a town no one gets used to, not even the natives."

"You're been there?" Skye asked, curious.

"Once or twice. Didn't stay long."

"Where are you from, Mac?"

He pushed back in his chair and looked confused. Apparently her question was a difficult one. But then he said, "Nowhere in particular. You know how it is, I get around a lot."

Yes, she knew how it was. "Still, you had to grow up somewhere," she persisted.

"Sure. Actually I grew up on a farm right here in Oklahoma."

"Really?" she asked, more interested than ever.

"Yep. Way out in the panhandle."

"What happened that you left?"

He became thoughtful once again. "Nothing in particular," he finally answered. "Kids grow up and leave home," he said, as though that explained everything.

"But what about you?" he asked, and leaned into the table, closer to Skye. "Why'd you leave Prospect?"

"Kids grow up and leave home," Skye mimicked.

He was half-naked. Again. Only this time Mac hovered just outside the back door nailing loose slats on the porch, where Skye couldn't help but look at him every time she crossed in front of the kitchen door. Bad enough that she'd had to watch him earlier in the afternoon when he mowed the lawn. At least then he was farther away, but now the life-size man worked a scant few feet from her.

Damn, didn't he know better than to parade around like that? Skye silently accused as she headed for the cupboard to collect pepper for the shaker. She'd forgotten to get it on her last trip to the cabinet for salt.

"Are you about done?" she snapped.

Mac gave her a curious glance. "Am I bothering you?"

"It's the noise," she thought to say. "It's driving me crazy."

"Sorry." He set the hammer down. "I'll do this another time."

"Good," Skye muttered. "Anyway, the Bensons will be here soon, and I expect the Lipcots will be dropping off Ali any time now. Why don't you go clean up before dinner?"

"Good idea." He reached for his skirt, which hung from the doorknob, and shook the dust out of it.

"I've got some clothes you can borrow," Skye offered.

He came inside. His eyes immediately flicked to her chest. "Think those skimpy little tops you wear might fit me, do you?"

Skye chuckled. "Not my clothes. My father's."

"Oh?"

"He died a long time ago," Skye said, responding to the question she saw in his eyes. "But I still have a few of his things." Her gaze went up and down Mac's length. "He wasn't so tall as you, or as . . ." *Muscled, sexy,* she thought, but said, ". . . as trim, but he was pretty big, and his things ought to do well enough for working around here."

"And they're probably softer," Mac said with a knowing grin.

Skye couldn't help her own smile. "Yes, softer," she agreed, realizing that one of the reasons Mac kept removing his shirt was that she'd ruthlessly stiffened the cotton fabric of his clothing.

Mac followed her to the cedar closet on the second floor, where she found a few suitable garments. "I washed everything before putting them away," she told him, "although they have been sitting in here for a long time. Maybe I ought to run them through the washer."

"No, don't do that," he insisted, and pulled the clothing out of her arms. "I'm sure they're fine."

Skye stifled a smile. He probably feared another starch attack. "Anything you say," she said cheerily, and went downstairs while he stalked off to his room.

Forty-five minutes later, she was in the kitchen with Ali when he entered.

"Well?" He hovered in the doorway, his arms outstretched, palms open.

Skye inspected the faded cotton shirt that fit fine through the shoulders but billowed through the midsection, and the old jeans that loosely draped his legs. "You look fine," she said with a straight face.

Ali, however, chuckled. "You look funny."

"Thanks a lot," Mac returned with feigned indignation, and moving next to Ali, playfully poked her in the ribs, causing her to squeal.

"At least it's a change of clothes," Skye cut in, "and that's more than you had when you got here."

Ali shot Skye a sour look, and Mac eyed her suspiciously. What had made her say such a thing? She wasn't a cruel person and took no joy in downing anyone. With Mac, however, she had to keep reminding herself of who and what he was, and maybe that's why she'd spoken so harshly. Still, she regretted her outburst.

"Sorry," she said, giving him a penitent glance.

"No problem," he said, and then he was smiling again.

Skye handed Ali a large tray filled with plates. "Take these outside and set the table," she instructed. "The Bensons will be down any moment."

Ali did as she was told, and Skye turned her attention on Mac. "Any good with a grill?" she asked.

"So-so," he answered with a tilt of his head and a lift in his brow.

"Good enough," Skye said, and handed him a spatula. "The ribs and chicken need turning."

"Yes, ma'am. I'll get right on it."

Mac cooked the meat to perfection, and Skye's salads were appreciated by all. The meal was eaten outside in the shade of several southern maples that had leafed a few weeks earlier. The afternoon temperatures were a little above average for April, but not hot enough to be uncomfortable, and everyone seemed to enjoy the barbecue.

After dinner, both Ali and Mac helped Skye clear the picnic table while the Bensons went back to their relatives' house for an evening visit. Once the kitchen was put in order, Ali went to telephone a friend, and Mac took up residence on a porch chair, while Skye put on a pot of coffee.

When the coffee had brewed, she stepped to the door to offer Mac a cup. Long shadows of dusk stretched the length of the yard, and the low sun was on the verge of disappearing for the night. Mac wasn't there. Searching the area, she found him at the far corner of the yard, a place where her father had hung a swing from an old elm tree many years ago. A ladder leaned against the stout trunk, and Mac was climbing.

He was on the last rung when she neared. "What are you doing?" she asked, looking up at his backside.

"Checking out something I noticed before," he answered without looking down at her. His attention was focused on the branch that held the rope swing. Using his weight, he pressed down on the limb several times, then reached for a thinner branch and worked it until it snapped away from the tree.

"Exactly like I thought," he said offhandedly after

eyeing the broken twig. He started down the ladder. Skye stepped aside, making room for his descent.

"Have a look," he said once he was on the ground, and handed her the twig.

The broken nub looked soft, pulpy. "It's rotting," she said.

"Better take that swing down before the branch breaks and someone gets hurt."

Skye stepped forward and curled her hands around the rough rope that held the weathered swing. Closing her eyes, she pictured herself on the seat, her father gently pushing and both of them laughing.

"Good memories?" Mac had moved behind her and stood so close, she heard his steady breathing.

"Yes," she answered. "The best.'"

"I can move the swing to another tree," he offered, sounding hopeful.

"Let's do that," Skye agreed, but knew it wouldn't be the same. "I knew the tree was in distress," she confessed. "A year ago I thought to move the swing and cut down the elm, but I put it off."

Mac's hand came to her shoulder, causing her pulse to skip. "It doesn't have to be done right away."

She turned, and his hand fell from her shoulder, but she found herself staring up into his hazel eyes, filmy with tenderness. "I've put it off too long," she said in a near whisper, the words choking out from her suddenly dry throat.

There was a moment of uneasy silence. Skye wanted to move away from Mac, but his gaze pinned her in place as though she were powerless over her own limbs. All she could do was stare into the depths of his eyes.

His lips parted ever so slightly. One corner lifted in a provocative gesture. Skye's breath caught. They stood so close, almost touching but not. Then his lips met hers and she gasped. His kiss was light and feathery, but hot, definitely hot. Her lips parted in invitation, and his kiss hardened as his tongue explored the soft lining of her mouth.

His arms circled her, and she gave no resistance when he pulled her into him. She loved the hardness of his chest, and grew heady with the feel of his quickened heartbeat and ragged breathing. Skye had never guessed anyone could affect her like Mac, drive her to such heights of wanton desire.

She wanted him.

Wanted him so much that she thought she might burst from a longing so great that every cell in her body seemed to be throbbing in desire.

His lips left hers, but his arms still held her in place. Her legs had turned to putty and her head spun. She shouldn't have let him kiss her. She ought to get away from him right now. But she was unable to move. Or maybe she didn't want to. Either way, when his head bowed and his lips parted for another taste of her mouth, she yielded instantly, then kissed him back. And kissed him good.

FIVE

The next day, Sunday, Skye told Mac he needn't perform any chores or make repairs. He'd worked hard and deserved a rest, she had insisted. She and Ali attended early services in Lindsay, Ali staying behind to enjoy a spring picnic for teenagers sponsored by the church.

When Skye returned to the inn, she spied Mac outside. Wearing a pair of loose-fitting coveralls she'd lent him, hammer in hand, he hunkered over the porch, pounding nails into newly shaped and placed slats.

Her high heels clicked against the wood as she walked the length of the porch. "The work will be here tomorrow," she said over the pounding of the hammer.

Mac lifted his head to look at her. Three or four nails were clamped between his teeth, their long shanks sticking out of his mouth, but when he saw her, he pulled them away and rose to greet her. His gaze roved her length, his hungry expression complimenting Skye more than words ever could.

"You're beautiful," he finally said.

She gave him a pleased smile, glad she'd chosen to wear the short print sundress with the sweetheart neckline. "Feels good to wear a dress once in a while," she said.

"You look spectacular in anything," Mac insisted, with a sure quality in his tone.

"Thank you, sir," she said on a playful half curtsy. "But why aren't you taking some time off like I told you to?"

Mac collected the hammer and nails and kneeled on the porch. "I'm planning on it," he assured her. "It won't take more than an hour to finish up here."

Seeing that he was obviously determined to complete the job he'd begun, Skye headed for her room. The day was already warm and growing hotter. The forecast was for temperatures much higher than normal for late April. Her panty hose felt damp and clung to her legs when she pulled them off and slipped into a comfortable, but very worn, pair of shorts.

Leaving her hair piled high on her head, she collected several straying strands and smoothed them in place, but they revolted and immediately fell down around her face again.

Thirsty, she went to the kitchen and made a pitcher of iced tea. Two filled glasses in hand, Skye strolled out back to check on Mac's progress.

He was still on bent knee, his back to her, when she approached. "Time for a break," she said optimistically. "I've got a cool drink for you."

"One more minute," he returned absently, his concentration staying with a plank while he continued hammering. "There," he said seconds later, then turned in her direction. "All done, boss lady," he boasted, but his gaze locked on to her leg, then did a slow tour up her thigh, stopped momentarily at her groin area, and traversed down the other leg.

Skye fought the urge to tug at the ragged hemline of her cutoffs. A recent washing had shredded more of the material, turning them into micro-minis. Nervously, and for lack of knowing what else to do, she turned and surveyed the tools scattered about the porch. "I'll help you pick up."

Setting the tea on a low table, she bent from the waist and collected an empty box of nails, a handsaw, and a tape measure. "I'll just set these on the table," she got out before glancing over her shoulder and seeing his grin, one that spoke of blatant male lust. Skye realized the view she must have given him when she bent to pick up the tools. She ought to be embarrassed, or angry, or something. But she wasn't any of that. All she could think was how feminine his appreciative eye made her feel and how she tingled all over.

Skye stepped to the edge of the porch and perched on the railing while Mac picked up the glasses from the table and offered her one. "Where's Ali?"

"I left her in Lindsay. The church is holding its annual picnic, one where parents and all other grownups, except the pastor and his wife, of course, are prohibited from attending." Skye sipped at the rim of her glass. "I'll pick her up in a few hours."

"I'll do that," he offered. "It'll give me a chance to have a look around."

Skye clinked her glass against his. "Now, that's more like it," she applauded. "Everyone needs a little diversion."

"So right you are." Mac took a seat in a chair across from her and drank his tea, downing half the glass in a few quick swallows. "What about you?" he asked. "How do you plan on spending the day?"

"With Ali gone, I have to stick close to the inn," she said, sensing he might ask her to go somewhere, and torn between regret that she couldn't and annoyance with herself that she wanted to.

"Not much is happening around here," he pointed out.

"No, but I still need to stay in case an unexpected customer shows up looking for a room."

"Do you get more people as the season progresses?" he asked.

"I hope so."

"I suppose the interstate being built to circumvent Prospect hasn't helped business," he speculated between swallows of tea.

Skye nodded. "I remember when every room was occupied and the guest book was filled with reservations for a month in advance. Back then Prospect was a thriving community. It was never big, but the people here prospered."

"What changed it all?" Mac asked, sounding genuinely interested.

"Lots of things," Skye said, and thought about the events shaping the town's demise. "There used to be a boat sales and repair shop on the other side of the lake that drew lots of people to the area until they relocated to Oklahoma City."

"But the lake is still here, and aren't there lots of other bodies of water in this vicinity?"

"Sure," Skye confirmed. "Since you're a native Oklahoman, you know the entire state is filled with mile after mile of shoreline, which includes lots of lakes for boating and fishing. But these days the larger ones, like Eufala, are the rage. We simply can't compete. Not as things are."

"With advertising you might draw some people," he offered.

"Maybe," she hedged, but knew he had a legitimate point. Her father had thought to do that very thing, but died first. Skye had barely finished college when he fell victim to his first stroke. The second one, a year later, had taken his life. Soon after, Henry Walker came on the scene, and at first Skye had felt grateful to Henry because he gave her mother reason to live. Her mother had written Skye often, always touting the virtues of Henry and saying how well things were going at the inn. Not one word had been true. Her mother hadn't deliberately lied, she simply placed blind faith in Henry, always looking for a better tomorrow and never seeing the man for who he really was . . . an irresponsible man who took whatever he could from people, even from Skye's mother, a woman he professed to love. Under his supervision, Carson Inn suffered greater losses. Even the money Skye's father had left her mother was gone by the time Henry walked out of their lives.

Mac's glass thudding against the aluminum table brought her out of her reverie. She glanced over at him to see he was studying her.

"Tell me, Skye." He leaned forward. "What did you do in St. Louis?"

"I got a B.A. in business with a minor in marketing and went to work for a manufacturing firm. Assistant to the marketing manager."

"Why did you come back here?"

"The position wasn't what it was cracked up to be," she confided. "Then, too, I had a few problems." She hesitated and searched his eyes. He really wanted to know about her. Mac was genuinely interested.

As if sensing her reservation, he asked, "What kind of problems? I'd like to know."

"I met a man," she began. "He worked for a competing company, but early on we vowed to keep work out of our relationship." Skye paused and swallowed a lump forming in her throat. Mac's stare was intense as he listened. "I thought things were going along fine," she continued. "Then one day Kyle asked me to do some snooping for him. My company manufactured toys, and he wanted plans for a product that was still on the drawing board."

"What happened?" Mac asked when she hesitated.

"I wouldn't do it, of course." Skye abruptly stood and turned, facing the yard. Her stare was blank and hazy as she looked out over the grass and trees. "We broke up," she choked out. "A few weeks later, the plans were stolen, and eventually a finger was pointed at Kyle. But he ended up getting away with it."

"Your company didn't press charges?"

She shook her head. "No. Through his lawyer, he informed them about an accomplice—one of their own employees."

"You," Mac stated behind her, and sighed deeply.

"Me," she confirmed, and wound her arms tightly around her middle. "They didn't want that kind of scandal, so I got fired instead and the matter was laid to rest."

Mac muttered a curse under his breath. "You didn't fight it?"

"I hired a lawyer, but he wasn't optimistic. Said my relationship with Kyle made me look guilty. I had motive and plenty of opportunity. I wanted to proceed anyway, prove my innocence, except then I learned how sick my mother had gotten. Once I came home, I lost the taste for the whole sordid business." Not to mention she'd had so many other concerns at that time. All at once she'd had to face her mother's heart condition and the disastrous financial condition of Carson Inn.

"This is Ali's home," she went on to explain. "Mine, too. Even though I never pictured myself running the inn, once I came back, I knew I couldn't simply let go of it. My mother's wish was that I try to hang on to the old place."

Mac came up behind her, wrapped his arms around her waist, and pulled her close until her back was solidly pressed to his chest. Skye closed her eyes and lingered in his comforting hold. He was so solid, and she felt suddenly secure.

"My poor Skye," he said softly in her ear. "You've had quite a time of it."

She turned in his arms, her gaze catching his. "Don't feel sorry for me, Mac. I don't need pity."

"I didn't mean it that way," he said as an apology. "It's only that you've had a few hard knocks."

"Maybe that's the way life is," she muttered, her thoughts going to her mother.

"But what about the good times, Skye? Don't you believe in them?"

"Oh yes, absolutely," she returned insistently. "I just think you have to live life with your eyes open, know what you're bargaining for and getting into."

Mac's gaze darkened in question. Out of the blue he asked, "Did you love him?"

Skye detected a hint of something in his voice. Was it jealousy? *Love him*, she repeated in thought, her gaze skipping along his chest. "I thought I did, or at least could have. Our relationship was building, or so I believed. But then, I never really knew Kyle, didn't know what he was capable of, and I guess I'll never know if he set me up from the beginning or if his scheme was an afterthought.'' What she didn't tell Mac was that in his arms, Kyle's appeal dwarfed in comparison.

Her head tilted back until she was once again looking into the depths of his eyes. He looked back at her tenderly, but his gaze was filled with something else, too, and she instantly recognized it as desire. At least she knew who Mac was. There would be no surprises with a man like him. She wasn't kidding herself or letting herself believe that they had a future together, and she'd already given him credit for behavior a notch or two above Henry Walker's. And he was not a low-down snake like Kyle. Mac kept his bargains; physical labor wasn't a four-letter word to him; and in his own way, he was an honorable man.

He bent to take her receptive mouth. She moaned and held him fast when his tongue slipped between her lips. No, she wasn't fooling herself about Mac, but neither could she resist him.

"Put in ten," Mac instructed the wiry attendant at Morgan Gas, and felt for the bill in his pocket that Skye had given him for gas before he left to pick up Ali in Lindsay.

He didn't like taking the money from her in the first place. It wasn't difficult to see the hard times Carson Inn had fallen on, and he wondered at the state of her finances. But then, she thought of him as penniless, so he had little choice but to take her money. Then, too, she wasn't likely to accept what she would consider charity under any circumstances. However, it was his own precarious circumstances that rubbed him raw at the moment.

Playing the part of a poor drifter had started as a joke, one that he never expected to last longer than his stay in Prospect, and that was supposed to have been less than a day. The charade had grown and expanded along with his stay, and he had no idea how to get out of it. He longed to come clean with Skye. But how? And what would her reaction be?

"You must be that young fella that's helpin' out the Carson girls," the whiskered man inquired, his squinty gaze roving the car in familiarity.

Mac nodded. "News travels fast."

"Prospect's too small a town for many secrets," he said, and winked. "Glad to see a man 'bout the old place again."

Mac was about to say he wouldn't be staying long, but didn't. The thought of leaving, never seeing Skye again, made his stomach clench, so he gave the man a polite smile instead. "Got a phone?" he asked, and was directed to an outside booth.

Having little change, he called his office collect, and a minute later his assistant came on the line and filled Mac in on the latest at Morgan Enterprises.

"Do the deal," Mac ordered when Roger told him about a counteroffer on a high-rise business complex they'd been negotiating for. "And, Roger, thanks for obliging my request that you don't call me at Carson Inn," Mac said, making reference to the message he'd left on the office recorder Saturday morning.

There was a moment of hesitation on the other end, then Roger said, "I don't understand why I can't call you, but you're the boss."

"It's complicated. I'll explain when I get back."

"When will that be?"

Mac shuffled uneasily and cleared his throat. He knew he couldn't stay in Prospect more than a week, give or take a day, but he wasn't prepared to pin down his departure from town. From Skye. "I'll let you know," he finally said, then added, "In the meantime I'll call you whenever I can."

The station attendant had completed filling the wagon's gas tank when Mac returned to the car. After paying the man, he headed east on the interstate and, per Skye's directions, exited at Southtrail Road, following it the rest of the way into Lindsay.

The church was on First Street, and he parked the car near the front door. Teenagers strolled the lawns, their chatter reaching his ears. He scanned the area, looking for Ali, and saw her talking to a group of kids on the front steps. She spotted him and waved.

"Mac," she greeted with a huge grin when she neared the car. "Skye was supposed to pick me up," she said, opening the door and settling in the front seat. "I'm glad you came instead."

"My pleasure, young lady."

He started the car up the street. "Have a good time?" he asked.

"Yeah, it was great," she responded enthusiastically. "I just wish some of my friends lived closer so I could see them more often."

"Aren't there any kids your age in Prospect?"

Ali shrugged. "There's Dan Cotter, but he lives on a farm a few miles from us and is always busy helping out his father. And there's a couple of others, but that's all."

"Think you'd be happier living in Lindsay?" Mac queried, wondering how attached the girl actually was to Carson Inn.

"No," she answered quickly. "I couldn't imagine living anywhere else. I'd like it if some of the kids moved to Prospect, that's all."

"Oh, I see."

"Skye says we might have to move, and I ought to get used to the idea."

"Does she now?" Mac gave her a sideways glance.

"Mmmm. But I don't believe it."

Skye's money situation was as bad as Mac had guessed. It had to be if she considered moving a possibility, since she'd been positive about her desire to keep the inn. If she had to give up on the place, the change was certainly going to take its toll on her and Ali. His heart ached for both of them.

"New places and meeting new people can be fun," he said, testing the waters, but saw the instant shake of her head in response.

"No, thanks," she said in a huff. "Not that I'd mind traveling a little," she added. "Long as I can always come home."

"You never know. One day you may want to leave home."

She seemed to give that some thought, and after several seconds, said, "I guess that could happen, and I do want to go to art school," but was quick to add, "I'd still want a home to come back to, and the inn has been in our family since my grandpa opened it a long time ago. Pa was always saying that the inn was our life, part of the family like a person."

Mac turned the station wagon onto the interstate, his mind filled with thoughts of Skye, the realist, trying to deal with Ali, the dreamer. He understood Skye's concern about her sister's distortion of the facts and wished he could think of something to say to Ali that might help the situation. Evidently Skye was carrying quite a burden, made heavier by Ali's staunch resistance to any alternative other than the one she perceived.

"Anyway," Ali was saying, "you're here now. Everything will be okay."

Mac recalled Ali's dream, or vision, or whatever she'd called her fantasy, that he was going to swoop in like some sort of superhero and save the day. The fact that Ali predicted his wealth and described his features niggled his sense of reason, and beyond that, more and more he found himself yearning to be the knight in shining armor she had conjured up in her mind. But a relationship, let alone a permanent one, with Skye was far from a reality, although he couldn't say he didn't like the notion. No, it wasn't right for Ali to count on him, and he couldn't be responsible for a young girl's dreams.

"Ali, what if I'm not who you think I am?" he tentatively asked.

"You're not," she responded matter-of-factly.

"I'm not?"

"Well, I mean you are, but not quite."

"How's that?" he asked, unable to conceal his confusion.

"You were supposed to be rich. At least that's how I saw you, but you're not, are you, Mac," she rambled on, "so I suppose that means you will be sometime or other, 'cause I saw you that way."

"Oh," was all he managed, and he brought his hand to his mouth to conceal a smile. Ali was something, all right, and, like big sister, quite a handful.

They drove the next minutes in silence until Mac turned off at the exit that would take them into Prospect.

"Skye really likes you," Ali announced when they neared the edge of town.

"I like her, too."

"She might not show how much she likes you," Ali warned, "but take it from me, she does."

Mac didn't need Ali to tell him that. Skye's kiss and

the way her body responded every time she was in his arms spoke volumes about her feelings. But did her feelings run deeper than the obvious physical pull they had to each other? And what about his feelings? How deep did they run?

He thought about how she'd confided in him about her tragedy in St. Louis, and a wave of anger washed over him. He didn't know what he'd do if he ever ran into that Kyle jerk. Having been betrayed himself, Mac knew all about the deep pain she'd suffered. If he hadn't fallen victim to a conniving woman, he probably wouldn't have understood how she could have been so gullible. From his own experience he knew how easy it was to be taken in by a pair of loving arms and soothing words. Before their marriage, his wife had been everything he always thought he'd wanted in a lifetime mate, and he never guessed she'd been playing a part. It had taken a few years of wedded hell before he finally realized the truth. She'd married him for his money.

At least Skye had escaped the trauma of a bad marriage and a hellish divorce. Still, she'd suffered, and he could understand why she didn't believe in miracles or happy-ever-afters. Hanging on to dreams was a hard thing to do in the face of so heavy a reality. He, too, was a realist, believing people made their own luck, charted their own futures. Nonetheless, there was something to be said for timing. Being in the right place at the right time had been the impetus that earned his initial fortune.

Mac glanced over at Ali and thought he wouldn't mind believing in dreams, particularly if they involved one luscious blue-eyed blonde and her saucy little sister.

Skye was in the front yard when they arrived. She

bent over the flower bed, a bunch of cut daffodils in one hand, a pair of clippers in the other. His gaze immediately flew to her rear end, which jutted upward, the rim of twin cheeks poking out from the bottom of skimpy shorts, their curved softness contrasting with the rough denim.

Hearing their approach, she straightened and stepped to the car. "Have a good time?" she asked Ali, and put a loving arm over her shoulder.

"Great."

"Thanks for picking her up," she told Mac over the white metal roof of the old station wagon.

"Any time," he assured her, and breathed in huge chunks of air in an effort to counter the effects she was having on his body. Damn, she was sexy, he thought as he followed them inside, his gaze riveted on the graceful movements of her shapely legs and the sway of her hips in motion.

Maybe Ali's dream would come true.

And his own in the process.

SIX

Skye completed her morning chores by eleven. She'd gotten Ali off to school, opened and manned the store for two hours, cleaned the Bensons' vacated suite, and changed the sheets in Mac's room.

Swiping at the perspiration netting her forehead, she headed for her bedroom and a change of clothes, and contemplated clicking on the air-conditioner. The unseasonable heat wave lingered on, and she was warm from the record high temperatures and the frantic pace she'd kept all morning. The thought of skyrocketing electric bills so early in the season kept her from doing it. At least the temperature had dropped during the night, so she was confident the Bensons' last evening had been a comfortable one, but now, with the inn devoid of guests, she couldn't justify the additional expense of cooling the large old house.

Rummaging through her drawers, she selected her oldest T-shirt and coolest cotton shorts. At any moment Mac would return from the paint store in Lindsay, and Skye wanted to dress as comfortably as possible when she helped him paint the porch. She'd changed, washed her face, and bunched her unruly hair in a high peak that bobbed atop her head as she walked, when someone knocked at her door.

Mac's warm smiled greeted her. "Are you ready to go to work?"

"As ready as you are," she replied, eyeing the coveralls he wore. They'd been her father's and were so old that the material was threadbare in spots, and discolored blotches appeared here and there.

Mac looked down at himself. "Is it okay to wear these?" he asked, responding to the way she'd inspected his garb.

"Of course," she answered absolutely. "I was thinking that those old coveralls have seen better days, is all."

He nodded his agreement. "I'm going to the shed for the brushes," he told her. "Paint's already on the porch. I'll meet you outside."

"I'm right behind you," she said, closing her door and following him down the hall.

"Sure you want to help out?" he asked with a glance over his shoulder.

"My appointment book is empty for the rest of the day," she chirped, "so I think I've got some time on my hands and ought to do something productive with it."

He shot her a devilish wink. "With you helping out, I can think of lots of productive things to do with my hands, but none of them have much to do with painting."

"I'll make sure you keep your mind, as well as all your body parts, on the task at hand," she assured him, with more confidence in her voice than she felt.

His chuckle was thin and full of challenge. "We'll

see." Then he was out the back door and making his way toward the work shed.

In his absence Skye collected some rags and set them out on the porch, then pried off the lid on one of the containers of paint that was labeled "country blue," the same color that currently adorned the wood slats of the porch. Mac had been right about being unable to match the old with the new, she noted, eyeing the creamy paint in the can, comparing the shade to the faded hue of the porch.

She churned the paint with a wooden stirrer and heard Mac's footsteps behind her. He set aluminum trays and brushes on the porch.

"Some for you," she said, pouring paint into the first tray, then a second, "and some for me."

"I thought we would share," he said, and gave her a wicked grin.

"No way." Skye visualized his hands working on her instead of the wood slats. She shook her head in an effort to shrug off the images forming in her mind, and passed him one of the trays and a brush. Pointing to the other end of the porch, she ordered, "You start there, I'll work here, and we'll meet in the middle."

"And if I object?"

"Hey, who's the boss here?"

"Right." He reluctantly went to where she had motioned. "Guess this is going to be one helluva quick paint job," he threatened. "Got to get to that middle fast."

Ninety minutes later, the space between them had narrowed by little more than several feet. Skye stood and stretched. "Whew. This is a bigger job than I thought."

Mac rose then, too. "It's a wide porch," he observed.

"Yes, and it looks bigger from a crouched position."

"How about a break?" he offered. "And a beer." When she gave him a puzzled look, he added, "I took a six-pack from the store, left the money on the counter."

"In that case, I'd love some, but you didn't have to pay. The least I can do is provide the beer."

"Next six-pack's on you," he said on a wink, then disappeared in the house, returning seconds later and handing Skye a can. She cupped it in her palms, the cool dampness of the aluminum against the heat of her skin a relief.

She followed Mac's lead and sat next to him on the steps. "You're a good worker, Mac," she praised, thinking of all he'd already done in the short time he'd been at the inn.

"I'm glad you feel you're getting your money's worth." He drank from the can in big, thirsty gulps.

"Maybe I could pay you," Skye told him. "It wouldn't be much, but I think you deserve more than room and board."

He pinned her with a stern look. "We made a deal. I see no reason to alter the conditions."

"But you're such a hard worker and—"

"And that surprises you?"

She shrugged and eyed the ground. "I didn't know what to expect."

"Long as you're happy, I've got no complaint," he insisted.

"I heard from one of my store customers that Jack Farrell is looking for help."

Mac's expression was full of surprise. She watched his throat work as he swallowed hard. "And?" he said at last.

"Jack lives in Prospect but has clients all over the county. He does landscape work mostly, but also sells and sets up lawn buildings. You know," she went on quickly, "sheds, cabanas, prefab garages and rooms. I hear he pays pretty well, and I thought you might want to check it out."

"Me?"

"Why not?"

"Ummm, well . . ." He hesitated. "I have a job."

"But working for Jack would be permanent, and you'd make some money," she persisted, and studied his features, hoping to spot some interest on Mac's part.

"That's not for me," he said firmly. "But thanks for the thought."

Skye's heart thudded in her chest, the hope that Mac could be tempted to take up permanent residence and a stable job dying inside her.

There was nothing to be accomplished by pursuing the subject, she told herself. He was a round peg that she was trying to squeeze into a square hole, and it simply wouldn't work—ever. She should have known better than to even try. She did know better.

"Think we'll get this done today?" she asked in an effort to clear her mind of foolish notions.

He measured the undone area with his eyes. "Guaranteed. Let's just hope it doesn't rain."

"Oh, it won't," she said with confidence. "No wet weather is expected in the foreseeable future."

"Ha. This is Oklahoma, and you know what they say. . . ."

"If you don't like the weather," she chimed in, "wait an hour."

"You got it."

She sipped from the can and glanced at the shadow slowly creeping down the side of the house. "At the moment I'd settle for a little shade, but it'll be another hour before it covers the porch."

Mac studied her face. "You're getting a burn. Doesn't look bad, but you ought to get something on it. Do you have any sunscreen?"

"Good idea," Skye agreed, and went to track down the lotion.

"You could use some yourself," she said on her return, and held out the plastic bottle after pooling some cream in her palm.

"No, thanks," he said with a wave of his hand. "My skin's adjusted to the sun. I don't need any."

"Then what's that little patch of funny color on your nose?"

His finger instantly went to the spot she stared at. "Where? What?"

"It's sunburn, all right," she said on closer inspection, and dipped her index finger in the cream she cradled in her other hand.

He eyed her raised hand suspiciously. "What are you going to do with that?"

"This," she said, and at the same moment, streaked the length of his nose with the lotion and giggled when he attempted to pull back but didn't quite make it in time.

"So," he said in a huff. "You going to sit there and laugh or complete the job you started?"

Skye wasn't about to refuse his challenge. She bathed her fingers with the sun block until mounds of lotion peaked on each hand.

In one quick, sure move she smacked his cheeks with the palms of her open hands, leaving a thick icing of white on his skin. "Oops, I missed a couple of spots," she proclaimed, and then his forehead and chin were also coated with a thick covering.

Mac blinked and brushed at his brow when a glob of lotion fell on his lashes. Another dripped from his chin onto the beer can in his hand. Skye tried to stifle her laughter, but seeing his fixed stare, looking both surprised and doleful, she couldn't restrain her throaty chuckles.

"Think it's funny?" he asked, and all she could do was nod and laugh harder.

"Then I know you'll think this is amusing." He set his beer can on the porch with a thud and clutched the sun block bottle.

"What are you going to do?" Skye watched him heap the lotion into his hands. He smiled at her fiendishly, his eyes gleaming in diabolic anticipation.

She jumped to a standing position and started backing up. "It was a joke," she pleaded when the bottle burped and gave up the last of its contents.

"Yes, ma'am, and a fine joke it was, too," he mocked.

When he stood and slowly came toward her, Skye had no doubt about his intention. "Now, wait a minute," she said with as much command as she could muster under the circumstances. "You don't want to do that." At that moment another big drop of lotion cascaded down his face, this one falling from the tip of his nose and catching on his lower lip.

He temporarily halted his forward march and tongued the white substance. "Mighty untasty," he declared, and started for her again.

"We ought to get back to work," she tried to reason. "I'll get a towel and clean all that stuff off you," she added for good measure, but it was no good. From the determined look in his eyes, she knew she was in trouble.

She turned to run, but it was useless. Like some huge

snarling bear, he was instantly on her, his full height towering over her and his strong arms cinching her waist, pulling her into him, his villainous laughter filling her ears.

"No," she managed to shout between choppy breathing, and put all her weight into pulling free from his hold. She felt him give an inch and thought she might get away, but in the next moment she fell to the ground, with Mac still attached to her.

He landed next to her. His arms cushioned her fall and he lay on his side with one leg ensnared between her knees. During the fall, he'd apparently opened his palms, and the sun block was smeared in a wide line covering the lower portion of her blouse.

Mac lifted a hand in inspection, then eyed the mess streaking her shirt.

"Are you happy now?" she got out between chortles, knowing the sight the two of them must make.

"Not quite." He dotted her face with a dozen white blobs. "I am now," he boasted when he was done.

Mac's laughter died slowly. The longer he stared into Skye's eyes, the less humor he found in the situation, since kissing her was fast becoming the priority of the moment.

Skye examined her shirt, then his face. "Guess we're even," she said, swiping at the cream clinging to his jawline and nose.

"I give if you do."

She nodded her agreement.

Mac gently rubbed away the creamy white spots on her cheek. Satisfied, he fingered errant strands of her hair, loving the way it curled and twisted in all directions, each lock seeming to have a will of its own. And her eyes . . . He adored her eyes. Filled with laughter, they seemed bluer than ever. Her mouth. Enticing. Inviting. His gaze lingered there, and he thought he might go crazy when her tongue lazily licked her lower lip.

Pressing closer to her, he tensed and felt his organ stiffen into a pulsating shaft of desire. Did Skye have any idea what she did to him, or how much he longed to have her?

He kissed her, savoring the sweet taste of her lips, and heard her breath catch when his hand touched her skin. When she brought her arm around him and pulled him tightly to her, he thought he would explode with longing.

He'd never wanted a woman like he wanted Skye, and his need for her was more than mere gratification of sexual urges. He would never be able to leave her behind, relegate her to a vacation memory. Silently he hoped Skye was no more capable of forgetting him.

If he'd read her right, she'd mentioned the local job opportunity in the hope that he'd stay in town permanently. Of course, working for Jack what's-his-name was an impossibility, and sooner or later he would have to tell her why. But at the moment all he could concentrate on was the soft, warm feel of her skin pressed to his. He tightened his hold on her and kissed her savagely, until he knew he had to stop. In another moment, it would take an army to pull him off Skye.

Reluctantly he let go of her. Skye's cheeks flushed with desire, and she bestowed on him a smile that was so seductive, he knew he'd better put her out of his reach, otherwise risk losing control altogether. More than anything, he wished for the privacy of night, pictured the two of them tucked away in some secure place where they could get as carried away as they dared. The sun cooking his back served to remind him that they lay in the middle of the lawn, in the middle of the day. Someone might intrude, and that was the last thing

thing he wanted. Skye was too special to risk sharing her with anyone.

As if her thoughts ran along the same lines as his, she eyed him with regret before standing up. Mac followed her cue and rose. He swiped at the grass clinging to his pant legs and followed Skye back to the porch, where she handed him a towel, and took another for herself.

Mac took a step toward her. "Need some help?" he volunteered when she dabbed at remnants of cream clinging to her clothing and legs.

"I think not," she returned seductively. "Otherwise, we'll never get anything done this afternoon."

"Don't be so sure." He winked. "I suspect we'd get plenty done. The porch wouldn't get painted, but—"

"But nothing," she interrupted, and took up a position on the porch where she'd left off before their break. Refilling her tray with paint, she continued, "We have to get moving if we're going to finish the job today."

Mac stepped beside her and bent to collect the open can of paint. "I do believe in finishing a job started," he told her.

She shot him a knowing look. "So do I."

Every cell in Mac's body jumped at the prospect of continuing what they'd begun in the grass. "Careful," he threatened. "I might make you honor your words."

"I always keep my word." Her tone was heavy with sensual undercurrents that vibrated through him, but in the next moment she pointed at his side of the porch. "One job at a time."

"Yes, ma'am," he said on a salute, and put his hands and back into tinting the wood slats, all the while his mind working on a fantasy involving himself and

Skye and a bed and all the things he was going to do to her.

"Dibs on the doggy," Ali squealed.

Mac set the game board on the kitchen table while Ali counted out money. "The horse looks good to me," he said, taking the game piece from the box.

"Guess I'll be the iron," Skye piped in, and settled in a chair opposite Mac, watching him sort the property cards by color, then line them up in neat rows. She inhaled deeply, taking in the faint scent of soap wafting across the table. Painting the porch had taken the balance of the afternoon, but they'd finished just as the sun was setting. After a late dinner, Mac had gone to his room and returned with damp hair and a freshly shaved face. He wore clean clothes: the jeans and shirt he'd had on the first day she'd met him in her store. She had replaced the missing button and patched a hole in the shirt.

Had it been a mere few days since he'd entered her life? Watching his easy manner with Ali, listening to their bantering about who was going to win the game, made her think that anyone looking on would assume he'd been an acquaintance of many years. Skye had to admit that he'd quickly chiseled a place in her and Ali's daily routine. And knowing he was bound to leave one day did little to lessen his impact on her life.

Until Mac, she hadn't known how much desire she was capable of feeling for a man. When they kissed, she longed for more and more of him, and when she wasn't in his arms, her body ached for his touch.

"Your roll." Mac handed her a single die. "You've got to beat Ali's four in order to go first."

Skye threw a two. "I'm last." She feigned a whimper.

Two hours later, she handed over the deed to her last railroad to Ali, who glowed over her success at building her empire. "Looks like I'm out," Skye proclaimed, surveying the empty patch of tabletop that had been filled with play money minutes before. "You broke me."

Ali turned her attention to Mac, who scratched his head in disdain. "You're vicious," he teased.

Her laughter was malevolent as she gloated. "You have to be to win this game."

Skye got up to fix them a snack of her homemade oatmeal cookies and pumpkin bread, leaving Mac and Ali to haggle over a property trade. "What happened?" she asked when she returned to the table and saw Mac looking dumbfounded at the game board.

"Your sister, the scoundrel, happened."

Ali stood and came behind Mac. She wrapped her arms around his neck in a loving gesture. "I'll be gentler on you next time," she promised.

"I bet," he challenged, but tenderly patted her hand.

Once the game board and all its various pieces were neatly set in the box, Skye passed a glass to Ali. "Milk for the winner," she offered, then handed Mac a cup of coffee and set one on the table for herself.

Mac took a couple of cookies from the tray and passed it to Ali. "These are great," he raved after downing one in a single bite. "Sinfully delicious."

"Thank you," Skye said. She'd baked them yesterday and had doubled the amount of chocolate morsels. Apparently Mac appreciated her efforts, and she silently admitted his approval was important to her.

Ali yawned. "I'd better get some sleep," she announced, earning a stunned look from her sister.

"Since when do you volunteer to go to bed?" Skye

asked, knowing her sister would stay up sketching pictures in her pad through the night if allowed.

"Since my school decided to set up an art exhibit in the entryway, that's when," she spouted. "I have to help haul things around and arrange the paintings, so I'll need all my strength."

"Mmmm." Skye suspected Ali was actually playing cupid by giving her and Mac more time alone.

"Will any of your pictures be on exhibit?" Mac asked Ali, who beamed at his interest.

"Oh yes. I'm showing three paintings," she told him in a very grown-up tone. "You can come with Skye on parents' day and have a look at them."

"I'd be honored."

"Great," Ali said, full of enthusiasm.

"Parents' day is a couple of weeks off," Skye said, directing her words mostly to Mac. From the downcast flicker of his gaze, he'd picked up on her meaning.

"Two weeks is a long way off," he said sadly. "I'll be gone by then."

"Mac agreed to stay and help us out for only a few days," Skye interjected, and tried to sound upbeat about the whole thing in spite of the sudden knots in her stomach at his words.

"Tell you what," Mac said to Ali. "If your sister can spare me for a bit, I'd like to stop around your school in a day or two and check out those paintings of yours."

Ali's eyes widened in joy. "You mean it?"

"You bet I do."

"You have to tell me before you come," she told him. "I want to give you the grand tour myself."

"Wouldn't want anyone else as my guide," he returned.

"It's settled then." Her eyes filled with adoration when she planted a kiss on his cheek.

Ali hugged Skye and said her good-nights, leaving Mac and Skye alone in the kitchen.

Skye motioned toward Mac's empty cup. "Want a refill?"

He pushed back in his chair and patted his stomach. "I've had enough."

Skye stacked the dishes. "I'll clean up then."

Mac followed her to the sink. "I'll help."

"There's barely anything to do," she insisted, wondering why she was suddenly feeling nervous. "I can handle it."

"I'm sure you handle most things well," he said to her back in a simmering tone.

Memories of the two of them clinging to each other in the grass filled her mind. So did her guarantee about finishing a job started. She set the dishes in the sink and shivered. Mac wanted to hold her to her word.

She glanced over her shoulder, her gaze trapped by his expectant one. Indeed he did. She made a half-hearted attempt at concentrating on the chore at hand, but it was no good. Goose bumps rose on her arms at his closeness. And when he nuzzled her neck, she dropped, rather than set, a freshly scrubbed saucer in the drainboard.

"This isn't helping," she said raggedly, her breathing growing more irregular by the second.

Mac lined her neck all the way up to her ear with delicate kisses. "Maybe not," he whispered. "But the dishes can wait. I can't."

His arms circled her waist and drew her buttocks into his crotch. The taut hardness of his length was a powerful aphrodisiac, and Skye trembled with longing.

"Did you mean what you said earlier . . . outside?"

he wanted to know, and Skye heard the catch in his throat as he spoke.

She turned in his arms. Her legs wobbled when she came face-to-face with the desire in his eyes. "I . . . I . . ." Her throat felt like sandpaper, and she couldn't find words to express how she felt. She wanted him more than she'd ever wanted any man, but Mac frightened her, too.

"Skye, I want you," he murmured. When she didn't respond, he took in a deep breath and set her apart from him. "To say I want you is the understatement of my life." His voice was a low rumble. "I don't know where all this is leading to, where these feelings will take us." A flicker of uncertainty shone in his eyes. "I want you, but it's up to you. More than that, I can't say."

"I haven't asked for promises of forever," she managed.

"No, you haven't." He stepped back and stuffed his hands in his back pockets. "But I won't hold you to something you said in jest."

Skye eyed the frayed tiles at her feet. "I told you," she said timidly. "I always finish a job."

Immediately and possessively he reached for her. "Are you sure?" he asked, his gaze turning a bright, glittering emerald.

"Oh yes."

His hand cupped her chin, drawing her gaze to his. She stared deep into his eyes, heady with the longing she saw there. Yes, she would finish what she'd started.

She'd done it now! Both relief and terror struck her all at once. She wanted to make love to Mac, and she'd admitted as much to him.

There was no turning back now.

SEVEN

Skye lingered in the kitchen doorway, took one final glance around the sparkling room, before turning off the overhead light. Heading for her bedroom, she hesitated at the staircase and looked up to the second floor.

Mac waited for her.

A combination of anticipation and nervousness made her pulse flutter wildly. She put a hand against her chest as though to calm her pounding heart.

She'd asked him to go up ahead of her, and although he'd seemed hesitant and shot her a questioning look, Mac had done as she'd asked without argument.

Continuing through the lobby and down the hall leading to the family's private quarters, she stopped at Ali's door. Her lights were off and all was quiet. A look inside confirmed that her sister was asleep.

Minutes later, Skye stood under the prickling spray of a shower. She let the water splash over her head and trickle down her hair for a long time. She wasn't stalling and wouldn't change her mind about what she and Mac were about to do, but she needed to take things slow. She wanted this special night to last, knowing she couldn't count on there being other times with Mac. Her chest tightened at the thought.

As if to throw off the sinking feeling, she shook her head. Large drops of water flipped from her hair to the wall of ceramic tile. Unlike her mother, she knew the score and wasn't kidding herself about Mac. She didn't expect to make a life with him, knew that he wouldn't settle down to one place, one job . . . one woman.

No. She wasn't her mother. Her eyes were open and she would handle the inevitable. All she expected was whatever the present offered, and she wasn't fool enough to let that get away from her, not when she wanted Mac so badly that her longing for him turned into a physical pain at times.

And . . . there was always the possibility that once they'd made love, her passion would cool. She turned her back to the water and palmed the wetness from her eyes. Ha! Fat chance of that happening, a little voice deep inside her whispered.

Finally stepping from the shower, she toweled the water from her body and blow-dried her hair, letting the long strands fall at will down her shoulders. Her body bristled in anticipation, the kind she remembered many, many Christmases ago when she hoped Santa would leave her a red bike. She hadn't been disappointed then, and knew Mac wouldn't disappoint her tonight. But would she be everything he hoped?

Studying her nakedness in the mirror, she conceded she'd been blessed with a good body. Her hips were full, but not nearly as large as her rounded, high breasts, and her waist was small. She possessed long, shapely legs and a taut, flat stomach. In spite of the endowments reflected in the mirror, doubts plagued her. She was as nervous as a schoolgirl anticipating her first kiss. She was being silly, she reprimanded herself. Then again, it wasn't as though she was an experienced lover. There'd been Kyle, of course. But the few times they'd been together hadn't exactly made the earth move.

What to wear? She eyed her clothes hanging in the closet and searched her drawers. What did one wear to a rendezvous in one's own house late at night? She debated between a lace and silk teddy, a floor-length cotton nightgown, and a pair of jeans and shirt.

The skimpy bit of silk seemed too predictable, a visible sign of forethought. But she was planning the night, she thought, admitting her rationale was on shaky ground. Still, the lingerie, even the simple cotton gown, made her uneasy, so she selected the jeans and long white shirtwaist blouse, but dispensed with underwear.

She wore no makeup but at the last minute decided on a dab of peach lipstick. Skye moved in on her reflection and locked gazes with the eyes looking back at her.

Suddenly she was terrified.

She'd never even had an orgasm.

A spasm of fear shot up her spine. How was she going to please a man like Mac?

To the window, to the door. Back and forth, Mac paced his room. Where was Skye? What was keeping her? Maybe she had changed her mind and wasn't coming after all.

He thought about what he might do, or ought to do, if she didn't show up. He'd spent years making hard business decisions, the kind lesser men shrank from, but one saucy blonde had managed to dissolve his backbone, leaving him spineless and incapable of knowing how to handle the situation.

He glanced at the clock. He'd left her downstairs an hour ago. She would come to him in a few minutes, she'd assured.

Mac rubbed at the growing stiffness in his neck. She wasn't coming.

Should he go to her? See what was keeping her?

And if he found that she had changed her mind, should he try to persuade her otherwise, woo the beauty to his bed, or act nonchalant—and that's exactly what he'd be doing, *acting*—and walk away as though her refusal meant little to him?

He stepped inside the adjoining bathroom and splashed cold water on his face. The window in his room was open, letting in the cool night breeze, but he was hot, his pulse was running a marathon through his veins, and the knot in his stomach kept tightening. Hell, he'd risked millions of dollars on deals without so much as a blink of an eye, but not knowing if Skye would show up had him in a panic. He didn't want to question why she was so important to him. He only knew she was, and deep down he sensed that this night would change his life forever, one way or another.

His gaze took in the suite, inspecting the preparations he'd made. One small lamp was lit, its dim light casting golden shadows through the room. He'd turned the bed down, fluffed the pillows, and made sure everything was neat and tidy.

Forlornly he eyed the door.

Skye wasn't coming.

But what was that? A noise drew his attention outside the closed door. He'd been at the inn long enough to be familiar with the sounds of creaking floorboards. He moved to the door and flung it open.

Skye!

Her eyes looked the slightest bit frightened, Mac

thought, and if his body was giving him fits while he waited for her, it was now in total panic as he faced her.

"Come in."

With a jerky shake of her head, she entered his lair. "I'm sorry I took so long," she apologized in a voice that was an octave higher than normal. At least he wasn't the only nervous one in the room, Mac consoled himself.

He picked up her scent. Clean and fresh, with no hint of perfume. Very Skye. He inhaled deeply. God, she was beautiful. Her hair hung loose, the way he liked it, and her long shirt ended halfway down her jean-clad thigh. When she turned and faced him, her breasts swung freely, and Mac felt the first strains of hardness pressuring his pants.

"I thought you might not come," he told her for lack of knowing what else to say. He hadn't felt this awkward since he'd kissed Mary Lou Parsons in the first grade.

"I . . . umm . . . had things to do." He watched the quiver in her lower lip as she spoke.

"Oh, no problem," he said a little too quickly, "I'm only glad you're here." Damn, he hadn't invited her for tea and crumpets, but from the strained politeness of their speech and airy courtesies, who would know different?

"Why don't you have a seat?" he offered, figuring they'd both relax if they got off their feet. He smiled at the notion. Wasn't that exactly the position he wanted her in? But when he looked at Skye, her glance went from the bed to the corner wing chair and back to the bed. Dilemma lined her features.

The chair looked comfortable and formal and . . . made for one. The bed, its coverings pulled all the way down, waited. The large mattress was definitely built for two. Skye crossed her arms in front of herself and held tight. Good grief! She hadn't been with any man in over three years.

Mac stepped behind her and roped her shoulders with his arms, drawing her to him. He chuckled, but the sound he made was tight, making Skye think she wasn't the only one who was nervous, and she found a measure of comfort in that knowledge.

"This is awkward," he stated softly, and she merely nodded. "Tell you what." He turned her in his arms until her breasts buffeted the hardness of his chest. Instantly her nipples hardened at the impact. His arms still around her shoulders, holding her in place, he continued. "I saw some wine downstairs. How 'bout I break open that bottle?" He pushed a few inches away from her and caught her gaze. "That is, unless you're saving it for a special occasion?"

"No, I'm not saving it," she mumbled, then managed a thin smile and added, "Anyway, I can't think of a more special occasion than tonight." She was rewarded with Mac's lopsided grin, and her heart leapt at the desire flaring in his eyes.

"Be right back," he assured her, and headed out the door.

Skye circled the room, eyeing the familiar furniture and walls that now seemed somehow foreign. Her fingertips stroked one of the oak bedposts at the bottom of the bed. Mac's bed. She finally settled in the chair, closed her eyes, and let the cool breeze that flitted through the window wash over her.

"Here we are," Mac announced with exaggerated cheerfulness as he entered the room. He carried a tray holding two long-stemmed glasses, the bottle of chablis, and a small bunch of Concord grapes.

Skye plucked a grape from its stalk and savored the taste while Mac poured the wine. He handed her a glass, then settled on the floor at her feet. "To us," he said in a toast.

"To tonight." She added her own version, once again reminding herself there was no tomorrow, and no "us." There was only now, if she could get over her case of nerves and take advantage of what was being offered.

Mac lifted her foot in his hand and gently kneaded her toes with his thumb, sending prickly little shocks up Skye's leg. Her breathing pattern matched the rhythm of his strokes.

"You've got great feet," he said in a hushed tone. "Beautiful feet," he corrected, then his fingers moved up her ankle and caressed the skin poking out below the hem of her jeans. He lifted her foot higher and set a kiss on the bridge of her toes.

Skye squirmed and stifled a moan of ecstasy. Her lids were heavy with pleasure, but when Mac rose and hovered over her, they widened in anticipation. In the next instant he lifted her in his arms, bringing her to a standing position, but it was his strength that kept her upright. Her legs had turned to jelly.

He held her tight. She set her head against his chest and listened to his rapid heartbeat. She lingered in his hold, content in the solid, strong feel of his body.

"Skye." He spoke her name reverently.

"Mac." She said his name on a whisper and looked up into his eyes. His gaze was shrouded in desire, and, in the dimly lit room, reflected dozens of emerald flecks that flickered seductively.

"Are you sure about this, Skye?" he asked shakily, giving her a final chance to break and run.

"Yes," she murmured, "but . . ." She hesitated.

"What is it?"

She avoided his intense gaze. "It's been a long time since I . . ."

She didn't finish, didn't have to tell him how long it had been since she'd made love to a man. He seemed to understand and drew her close to him again.

"It's been a while for me, too," he confessed, and tightened his hug. Mac's admission put Skye more at ease than anything he might have said or done, and made her feel special. Never mind that his sense of what constituted a long time probably didn't match her own. It was enough to know that he wanted her as much as she wanted him.

His lips parted, and she noticed that the lower one trembled a little. Slowly she tilted her head upward as he bent toward her. Her blood pulsed harder and harder until their lips met. The explosion of sensations that followed was more powerful than anything she'd experienced. His kiss was hard and charged with longing and anticipation, and she returned it in full measure. Somewhere deep inside her, a fire raged. All control lost, she gave way to instinct and some unseen force that was more insistent than anything she'd ever felt.

Mac's hands were all over her as though obsessed to know every line of her body. They pulled her in tighter and tighter and stroked her back, mapped her waist and hips, squeezed her rear end, petted her hair, and rubbed her shoulders, and Skye loved every second of his endless search.

Giving in to her own obsession to touch Mac, to know him, she let her hands drift down his hair. The strands were cool silk against her fingers. She traced a pattern down his neck, finding the spot where his pulse throbbed heavily, and she ran her hand the length of his arm, reveling in muscles that rippled and quivered under her touch.

With a moan, Mac pulled away from her. He pinned her with a gaze filled with craving. She thought he might say something, but there was no need. They spoke a silent language, one they both fully understood that required no words, only a look.

Her throat went dry and she was certain a thousand butterflies had lit in her stomach, but yearnings stronger than any attack of nerves made her reach for his shirt. With trembling fingers, she worked the buttons and drew in a ragged breath once the cotton cloth fell away from his skin and landed in a heap at his feet.

Fingers splayed, she pressed her hands against the flat of his chest and savored the warm feel of skin and muscle. Next she planted a kiss on each of his pectorals, first one, then the other. Each stiffened in turn under her touch. His moan of pleasure spurred her on to tackle his pants, and she drew a line with her index finger down his center, stopping at the ridge of his jeans.

"Do you know what you're doing to me?" Mac asked, his words coming out choppy.

Yes, she knew. One look at the huge bulge pushing against the fabric of his pants, and how could she not know? The snap at his waistband easily gave way. The zipper was no more of a problem, and Skye wouldn't have been surprised if the bits of metal found a way to sigh in relief from the pressure they'd endured the last few minutes.

She hooked her thumbs over the waistband of his jeans, catching his cotton briefs in the process, and tugged until they fell down around his knees. Mac helped by kicking off his boots and stepping out of his pants. Skye took a couple of steps back and inspected him. Her breath caught at his beauty. She didn't know men were beautiful, never thought about them in those terms, until now. From the first, that day she'd found herself in this very room and saw him lying naked on the bed, she'd been in awe of him.

Now she took him in fully, appreciative of the vee shape of his body, the rippling tautness of his flat stomach, his muscled legs, and, dear Lord, his magnificent maleness, all long and hard and pointing straight at her.

"My turn," he said, narrowing the space between them.

Skye froze in place. She couldn't move if she wanted to, but she didn't want to, even if she couldn't quell her nervousness. She trembled and closed her eyes when his hands reached for her shirt, the feel of his fingers working a path down the buttons driving her crazy.

She opened her eyes on Mac's gasp and saw he stared at her exposed breasts. "You're the most beautiful woman in the world," he said with such certainty that Skye actually felt she must be.

Mac pulled her into the circle of his arms, and their lips joined in a long, passionate kiss. His tongue entered her receptive mouth as his thumbs stroked the underside of her breasts.

Skye didn't know exactly when or how her jeans came off, but she was more than aware of Mac's hand exploring the inside of her thigh. Hot embers ran up and down her body, the heat growing in intensity every second. Then she was cradled in his arms. Gently he set her on the bed and lay beside her. His lips came to her breasts, and her nipples hardened even more when he kissed first one, then the other. Arching her back, she pushed toward him in an unspoken plea for more, and he obliged. His tongue drew wet circles around one stiff peak, and she thought no pleasure could be greater than when he took the nipple in his mouth and sucked.

"This one needs attention, too," he said, moving to the other breast, and Skye squealed and squirmed in pleasure as he heaped one delight after another on her.

When his mouth moved up to her lips, she let her hand rove his body. He was hard and warm all over, and his whole being seemed to vibrate under her touch. Her hand slid farther and farther down until she fingered the springy hair at the base of his sex.

"Touch me, baby," Mac breathlessly pleaded between kisses.

She grasped his sex. The hard shaft pulsed in her hand, and she wanted him inside her. Mac's hand came down on the mound of curls at the vortex of her legs. He stroked and teased and brought her to the pinnacle of desire.

"Mac, please," she begged, thinking she was going to shatter in a million pieces any second.

As though he understood her need, he wedged himself between her legs, and then, in one quick surge, he was inside her, filling her, and she hadn't known how empty she'd been until that moment. Back and forth they rocked, the tempo increasing until their breathing was heavy and ragged.

"Mac." Skye screeched his name, and on a heave the world exploded into a thousand fragments. The sensations controlling her body were like none she'd known. Release mingled with pleasure, and somewhere in the mix an uncontrollable urgency drove every sensation. She moved reflexively, her hips somehow managing to keep time with Mac's. He burrowed deeper and deeper inside her, then let out a loud moan and climaxed.

A new wave of wet heat filled Skye, but this time it

brought contentment and a conviction that all was well with the world. Mac stretched out on top of her, his body hot and damp and spent. On an impulse, Skye squeezed her womanly muscles, earning his startled but pleasured groan. But it was Skye who got the final surprise when he lifted his head and flashed her a wicked grin. His brow shot up provocatively, and suddenly his shaft grew inside her. She squeezed again and felt an extraordinary sense of power.

"The lady wants more," he taunted.

"And more, and more, and—"

He quieted her with a kiss . . . and more.

Movement made Mac stir. Reluctantly he opened his eyes and peered through the dark of the room to see Skye getting out of bed.

He caught her wrist as she stood. "Where are you going?"

"Shhh. It's the middle of the night," she whispered as though afraid someone might hear. "Go back to sleep."

Mac bolted upright instead. His eyes began adjusting to the dim light of his room and he saw that she had stepped into her jeans and was searching the floor for her blouse. With an appreciative eye, he watched her well-endowed breasts jiggle as she moved about the room.

"You don't have to leave," he said when she plucked her shirt from the floor and started getting into it. "Stay, please."

Skye finished buttoning her blouse, then sat on the bed next to him. "I have to go," she explained. "It'll be dawn in an hour, and I don't want Ali to see me coming from your room."

The light bulb went on in his brain, which at the

moment seemed a bit fuzzy, although he had no difficulty whatsoever remembering the feel of Skye under him or the degree of happiness he'd felt when he'd nodded off to sleep with her spooned against his body.

"Ali's very impressionable," she reminded him. "She'd make too much out of the whole thing."

Disappointment clutched Mac's gut. "She's not the only one who might make a big thing out of what happened between us," he told her, and instantly regretted the annoyance he heard in his voice. Surely Skye hadn't meant to imply their lovemaking had been a casual, one-of-those-things-that-just-happened one-nighter? She couldn't think that?

Even in the dark he made out her bewildered expression. "I didn't mean it like that," she said apologetically. "It's just that at thirteen, girls think in terms of forever and happy-ever-afters."

"They're not the only ones," he interjected, but she didn't seem to be listening.

"And you know about Ali's preoccupation with fantasy. Can you imagine what she would think if she saw us together—" she motioned at the bed "—like this?"

"Yep, I can imagine."

Skye lifted his hand in hers and smiled. "Last night was wonderful," she said sweetly. "Thank you."

Mac figured he'd just been taught a lesson. Now he knew what it felt like to be loved in the dark of night only to be left before the light of the day. Slam-bam-thank-you-ma'am never had so much meaning as it did at this moment. Only it wasn't dawn, and Skye's words of appreciation sounded heartfelt even if a little too final for his liking.

"You sound like we're never going to . . . umm, get close again," he said.

Her lashes lowered and her words came out softly. "I hope we do."

"Do you?"

"Yes."

He pushed back in the bed. Relief washed over him. "For a minute I thought we were history," he confessed. "And before we ever really got started."

She leaned into him and kissed him tenderly. "I didn't want you to think I expected more." She began her own confession. "Didn't want to make you feel obliged or—" she shrugged "—or anything."

His hand went to her cheek, its warmth and softness like satin against his newly callused skin. "Don't you know you could never make me feel that way?"

"I wouldn't want to," she said, sounding uncertain. "I want you to feel free to do whatever you want, come and go as you want—"

"Don't worry," he interrupted. "I do feel free to do all that. Believe me."

"Okay, I do," she said, but instead of looking relieved, she tensed and grimaced.

What was she so worried about? he wondered. On the surface she seemed concerned that he not feel penned in, but he couldn't think why she even considered that important or a problem. Maybe he was suffering her skepticism because of the experience in St. Louis. Sure. That was it. She'd been hurt badly and was a little gun-shy. Or—he didn't much like his next thought—she was trying to tell him that she didn't want to get too serious or tied down to a long-term relationship.

He was still pondering the notion when she gingerly kissed his forehead, then crossed the room. Taking care to open the door quietly, she turned and blew him a kiss. Mac pretended to catch it.

He watched her leave. Confused about what Skye

had been trying to tell him, and even more confused about where she saw their relationship going, he did know a thing or two about his own feelings. No woman had touched him the way Skye had. That was a definite. And he couldn't image his life without her in it.

EIGHT

"Mac!" Skye squirmed out of his hold. "Someone might come in."

Mac gave the empty store a cursory search. "Let them."

"Oh no, you don't," she said, her laughing eyes belying the seriousness of her tone. "You've no idea how fast gossip travels in this town."

"Let 'em talk," he said on a shrug, thinking that it felt more like days than hours since he'd held Skye in his arms. He'd managed a polite distance from her at breakfast since Ali was at the table, and when Skye had gone to open the store, he'd climbed the roof to check out the shape of the decaying tiles. From his high perch he'd watched several townspeople come and go, and knew the moment she was alone.

"How's the roof?" Skye asked, and he took it for an effort to dissuade him from his intentions.

"You need a new one," he replied, all the while steadily moving toward her while she kept pace with backward steps until her back pressed into the counter.

"Gotcha," he gloated, and took her in his arms. Before she could protest, he covered her mouth with his in a deep kiss. One she returned without a fight. He heard her sigh and felt her arms as they came up over his shoulders. Skye tasted like honey and smelled of spring, and he wanted to eat her up.

He let her go reluctantly. "Don't expect that to be the end of it," he warned. "My appetite's mighty fierce, and I consider that kiss an appetizer."

She put her hands on her hips. "Is that a threat?"

"No. It's fact."

"Hmmm. We'll see about that."

At that moment the bell over the door jangled and a thin, elderly woman with silver hair and a drawn face entered. Mac recognized one of Skye's regular customers. "Good morning, Mrs. Purdy," he greeted.

"Mornin', young man." She beamed and her face colored a bit. "And you, Skye. How you doin' this wonderful day?" She filled her lungs with morning air.

"Absolutely grand, Mrs. Purdy."

The old woman leaned into Skye and studied her face. "Hmmm. I'd say you'd been bitten by the love bug." She turned her attention to Mac, missing Skye's cheeks turn to scarlet. "Is this your doing, sonny?" She walked to where he stood near the door.

Mac cleared his throat. He wanted to laugh, but managed to subdue the impulse. "I sincerely hope so, Mrs. Purdy."

She playfully swatted his chest with the back of her hand. "You're a big one, ain't you? And a looker, too."

Mac only smiled.

"Why, if I was thirty, maybe forty, years younger, I'd give our Skylar a run for her money."

"And I'd be honored." Mac bowed at the waist.

"Mrs. Purdy," Skye, recovering from the woman's earlier bluntness, called from behind the counter. "What can I get you today?"

"Bread, two loaves, one white and one rye," the woman told Skye with a backward glance. "And a quart of milk, and tea. I ran out yesterday and forgot to pick it up last time I went shopping in Lindsay."

Mac kept one eye on Mrs. Purdy, who went on to list several additional items, and the other on Skye as she scurried around the store filling the order.

"I see you been doin' quite a few repairs around this place," Mrs. Purdy said.

"Yes."

"That's right fine. The old place could use a fixin', but if you intend to hitch up with our gal—"

"Mrs. Purdy!" Skye chastised, but the woman didn't so much as flinch.

"See here, Skylar Carson, I've known your mama since she was a little one herself, and since she ain't here to look after you, I figure the task falls to me."

Mac shrugged and gave Skye a helpless look. She shook her head and muttered something inaudible under her breath. Undoubtedly she figured arguing with the old woman was useless since she went back to gathering items from shelves.

Mrs. Purdy turned on Mac again. "As I was sayin', it's good you're fixin' up the old place, but Carson Inn ain't likely to earn 'nough to feed another mouth. Not on a regular basis, anyhow. I hear Jack Farrell is lookin' for a good man. He's my nephew, you know," she said with obvious pride.

"No, ma'am, I didn't."

"Be happy to put in a good word fer ya."

"Thank you, but I don't think that's for me." From the corner of his eye Mac noticed that Skye had stopped in place and was staring at him, and he thought he saw disappointment in her gaze. But then she was off again, dropping a few items on the counter and going after others.

"Can't say I understand that," Mrs. Purdy was saying. "But it's your decision. I reckon you ought to chew on it a bit more before sayin' no for sure." She became tight-lipped, and Mac decided he must have insulted her.

"I'll think about what you said," he offered, in an effort to placate the old woman.

She smiled thinly and stepped to the counter. "You do that, young man," she said over a sagging shoulder. "You just do that."

Mac backed out the front door. Mrs. Purdy had meant well, and under different circumstances, he might have jumped at a job. As it was, her concern for his finances wasn't necessary. Once again he found himself thinking about the dilemma he was in.

He was a drifter with a talent for making repairs, as far as Skye and the people of Prospect were concerned. The whole thing had started out as a joke, but more and more it felt like deceit, and he was beginning to see himself as the perpetrator of a big, bald-faced lie.

Of course, he hadn't known he'd end up staying in the small town more than twelve hours, plus or minus one or two. And he sure hadn't counted on the depth of his feelings for Skye.

He had to tell her the truth about himself, but needed to find the right time and place, and hope she would understand. He thought about the lake behind the inn. With its swaying trees, mossy banks, and rippling water, it was the perfect spot for a nice little tête-à-tête. He would just have to see what he could come up with to get Skye there.

In the meantime there was a roof to patch before the next rainstorm brought more damage. And later—Mac licked his lips in anticipation—there was Skye to take care of.

"How's it going?" Skye hollered, snagging Mac's attention. Her hand over her brow protected her eyes from the glare of the midday sun as she looked up to the roof.

Bracing himself against an eave, he stood and peered down at her. He wore no shirt, and his jeans rode low on his hip. His skin shone from a sheen of perspiration, and a constantly shifting breeze caught his rumpled hair and tossed it about. Skye swallowed the wad forming in her throat and wondered if she would ever grow immune to Mac's charms.

"I'm about done," he called, swiping the sweat from his forehead. "Be down soon. Make sure the beer's cold, 'cause I've got one powerful thirst."

"You got it," she called up, and went back inside to check on the beer stash and see about making Mac something to eat. He'd gone into Lindsay to purchase some roof patch, and began making the repairs as soon as he'd gotten back, working steadily since then without a break. She'd learned enough about him to know he must be starving.

Leftover fried chicken and a fresh garden salad ought to do, she thought, taking the food from the refrigerator, when she heard the bell jingle on the counter in the lobby.

"Afternoon, Skylar." Lester Drummond, Prospect's mailman, tipped his hat when she entered the room. "Got something special for you."

"Oh?" Lester rarely came inside the inn, but left the mail in the box at the road's edge.

"Must be important." He held up a clipboard. "You've got to sign," he informed her.

Who on earth would be sending her a registered letter? Skye wondered as she scribbled her name on the line Lester indicated. A cold spear of trepidation traveled up her spine as she speculated on the letter's origin. Mr. Dwyer at the bank had forewarned her of legal action. She'd known this moment was coming. Somehow she hadn't thought it would be so soon.

"Thank you," she managed to tell Lester, and tried on a smile, but suspected it looked more like a frown from the curious look he shot her. She clutched the envelope to her chest and waited until the mailman was out the door and down the porch steps before she dared check for the envelope's source.

She stared long and hard at the printed return address. "First State Bank of Lindsay," she read over and over until the envelope trembled in her hand. It wasn't good news, her knotted stomach told her, but she wouldn't know for sure until she opened the letter. On a long, deep breath, she did just that and stepped to a chair as she read the contents, glossing over all the perfunctory words, until her gaze fixed on the word "foreclosure," and her body dropped limply into the chair.

Through a blur of tears, her eye drifted to the amount due at the bottom of the page. So much money. And she had to come up with the entire amount of back payments plus penalties within ninety days or say goodbye to Carson Inn forever.

The inn had been bought and paid for decades ago, but Henry Walker had talked her mother into a mortgage. For renovation and expansion, he'd said, but little, if any, of the money had been used for its intended purposes. From what Skye knew about Henry, she suspected the money had been lost at poker games and horse races throughout the Southwest.

Skye shook her head as if to throw off her shroud of self-pity. *What ifs* did no good at all. What was done, was done, and she had to move forward, deal with the situation as best she could. Drawing a shaky finger to her eyes, she blinked hard and swiped at the little pools of liquid that collected at her lashes.

Milo Craft would come through for her and Ali. Surely he'd lend her the money to pay back the note. Even if time and events had distanced Milo from what was left of the Carson family, her father had always told her she could count on Milo, no matter what.

Skye thought back to the days when Milo was a constant visitor to Carson Inn. And there were the happy days she'd spent on Milo's ranch. He was the one who had taught her to ride a horse, she fondly remembered, and felt the tension flow out of her body. Milo would lend her the money. He had to. She forced a smile. Then another. In a few minutes she did begin to feel a bit better. And just in the nick of time. She looked up to see Mac walking through the front door.

"Job accomplished," he announced, but added, "at least for the moment. A whole new roof is going to be a priority real soon, though," he warned.

"I know."

Mac took a long, studying look at Skye. There was no hint of color in her usually rosy cheeks, and even though she smiled at him, there was no cheer in it.

"Is something wrong?" he asked.

"No, nothing," she answered, a little too quickly to be believed, and he wondered if now might be a good time for that fishing date he planned. Skye looked as though she could stand to wile away a few hours in the fresh air.

Stuffing the letter in her back pocket, Skye headed for the kitchen. "Lunch will be ready soon," she said, and noticed he followed close behind. "Leftover chicken, if that's okay?"

"You're making my mouth water."

"I like a man with an appetite."

"Then you must love me."

Skye nearly dropped the bottle of beer she'd taken from the refrigerator shelf at his use of the word *love*. Did she love Mac Morgan? The question poked at her heart until she felt little more than a dull, but persistent, pain. What she felt for him mattered not at all. She couldn't think in terms of love where Mac was concerned. No matter how she felt about him, she refused to let herself be swept into a false, make-believe world. Her mother had believed in, and wished for, the impossible, blinding herself to reality. Skye would never make that mistake.

"Well?" Mac stood at the table, waiting for an answer.

"What?" she asked, pretending to have forgotten his question.

She swept past the table and heard his sigh.

"We were talking about appetites," he said, and reached for her arm as she moved.

Stopping in place, she turned to look up at him. "Sorry. Guess I'm a bit preoccupied."

"I've got an idea," he said with renewed enthusiasm, and she was all too aware of the exact moment his hand fell from her arm.

"What?"

"A picnic and a little fishing. That lake behind the inn is brimming with bass. Are you game?"

"But the inn," she protested.

"Put out the 'gone fishing' sign. From what I know about the people of Prospect, no one will mind."

"That's true," she agreed, but sounded hesitant. "What if someone calls for reservations or, worse yet, stops in without them and finds the place closed?"

"Set up the telephone recorder. You can call people back."

Call people back? Sure! By this time Mac knew as well as she that there probably wouldn't be any calls to return, not from prospective guests at any rate. The likelihood that a potential customer would walk in off the street was even less likely, and she found herself grateful that he hadn't said as much. Sometimes he could be extraordinarily considerate.

"Ah, come on," he prodded. "We can both use a break."

"That's true." A few hours away from the inn and its problems was exactly what she needed. "Let's do it."

Minutes later, Mac, loaded down with two poles, a tackle box, and a blanket for spreading on the ground, and Skye, carrying a filled picnic basket, hiked the half mile to Prospect Lake.

"How about this spot?" Mac stopped at a mossy bank that jutted out into the water. An irregular row of spindly birch trees shaded the area. When Skye nodded her consent, he spread the blanket on the ground, then helped her set their lunch on top of it.

Mac ate gustily, and even Skye's appetite picked up as she watched him devour one piece of chicken after another. The day was perfect. A light southerly breeze kept the warm air stirring, and the cerulean sky was cloudless. The air was sweet, scented with the growth of spring.

"Which pole do you want?" Mac asked after he'd swallowed his last bite.

"You pick."

Skye cleared away the remnants of their meal while Mac tested the stringing on the reels, then set the poles and tackle box at the edge of the water. Skye joined him and picked up her pole.

The land abruptly dropped into the water at that spot. Skye sat with her legs dangling over the edge as she cast out her line, satisfied at its resting spot yards in front of her.

She caught the first fish and proudly put it on ice, then tried for another. For a long time they sat at water's edge, poles in hand, taking turns at successful catches until they had enough fish for a couple of meals.

"You're a natural," Mac boasted.

"It helps that the lake is brimming with fish."

Mac looked out over the water. "This is a fisherman's paradise," he asserted, making a mental note of the vacation possibilities such a spot held. When his glance fell on Skye, he saw she'd set her pole on the ground next to her. He followed suit, glad that the tint was back in her cheeks and her smile appeared genuine. Bringing her here had been a good idea, but he wondered if the moment was right for telling her about himself. He wished he knew what had been bothering her earlier. Should be burden her with the truth right this moment?

"It's been a great afternoon," Skye said. "I'm glad you talked me into coming." She leaned back on her elbows. "It's been a long time since I've been fishing."

Next to her, Mac stretched out on his side. "It's

peaceful here," he said in a hushed tone. "Great place to think."

Skye didn't want to think. All she wanted to do was enjoy the breeze that caressed her skin and inhale the fragrance of the wildflowers in bloom. But she couldn't entirely set aside her troubles, and even now the threat of losing the inn and disappointing Ali made her head spin.

"Something wrong?" Mac asked when she sat up and massaged her temple.

"No, nothing." She looked in the direction of the inn, its chimneys sweeping up to the sky. "We ought to get back." But when she began to rise, Mac clutched her arm, pinning her in place.

"Skye, I've been wanting to talk to you about something."

Curiosity flashed in her eyes. "What?"

Mac bolted upright. "Walk with me?" He hoped the movement would loosen the knots in his stomach and the ones binding his tongue. How to tell her? What to say? How to begin? Roger, his assistant, would have a great chuckle over his boss's loss for words and sudden lack of nerve. Though he was known in business circles as outspoken and direct, Skye had turned him into 180 pounds of insecurity.

He was about to say something. Anything, in the hope that the right words would come to him. But Skye chose the same moment to open up the conversation.

"I must have seemed a little down in the dumps to you earlier," she said, certain her mood prompted his suggestion for an outing. "But catching all those fat, lovely fishies has made my day."

Mac stopped walking and turned to face her. "Do you feel better?"

Her eyes met his. "Yes."

"What was wrong?"

"Nothing very important. A few business problems," she said on a shrug, fighting her growing desire to tell Mac everything.

"Anything I can help with?"

"No."

"Sometimes talking helps."

His gaze was tender, full of concern. Talking it out might help, make things clearer. She moved away from him and sat on a large, flat-topped rock a few feet from the shore.

Mac balanced on his haunches next to her. "I'd really like to know about it, Skye." Thoughts of his own confession completely left him as he saw the combination of pain and fright flit through her eyes.

"It's the inn," Skye began. "We could lose it."

Mac moved in closer until he'd settled next to her on the rock. He draped his arms over her shoulders and drew her close. "I know business is slow," he said.

"Like a graveyard," she said.

"How long's it been this bad?"

"Before I came home. Things just keep going downhill, and now the bank is foreclosing."

"There's a loan?" Mac asked, unable to hide his surprise. He knew the inn had been in the Carson family for a long time, and he'd assumed any mortgage was paid in full ages ago.

"My mother's second husband took it out."

He noticed she hadn't used the term *stepfather* or any endearment to describe the man who had married her mother. "Where is your . . . uh, mother's husband? Did he leave you holding the bag after your mother's death?"

"Long before that," she said, her words stumbling

out, and once again the color in her face paling. "He squandered the money, then left soon after. Mother died a few months later."

Mac found himself wanting this monster's name so he could track him down and give him a good thrashing for what he'd done to the Carson women, but at the moment his rage didn't matter. Only Skye was important. His hand stroked her arm as he waited to hear more.

"Milo Craft will help," she told him, explaining the relationship between the Carsons and her father's oldest friend. "He's out of town, but will be back soon. I should hear from him in a few days."

Mac recalled the name Craft from his boyhood days. Even then the Craft Ranch had a reputation as one of the leading horse ranches in the Southwest. "Sounds promising," he told her, but saw the doubt in her eyes and wondered how certain she actually was that Craft would come through for her.

I'm not sure about Milo's answer, Skye silently admitted. His long-standing kinship with her family had to mean something, but a nagging doubt persisted, and she knew it was because of his impersonal, hurried tone when she'd made her request.

"I know Ali can't imagine leaving this place," Mac said hesitantly. "But what about you, Skye?"

"There was a time when I didn't question leaving Prospect," she said. "But I always knew the inn would be here. Home would be here as it has been for generations. I never dreamt we could lose it." Her glazed eyes met his. "I can't let it go, Mac." Her voice was filled with desperation. "I can't."

Skye burrowed her head into his chest. Her tears ran freely. She hadn't once cried over her troubles, knowing tears did no good. But in Mac's arms, she couldn't hold back the rush of emotion any longer.

"It's okay, baby." He held her tightly and rocked. "Get it all out."

It would be all right, Mac silently vowed. He'd make sure of it. For the moment all he could do was provide whatever comfort she would let him give.

NINE

Hinges squeaked with each forward movement as Mac slowly rocked back and forth in the old bench swing on the back porch. He made a mental note to oil the workings, then went back to studying the colors of a brilliant sunset. Hues of gold and burnt orange filled the western sky. There was a special kind of tranquility in the minutes before dusk, as though Mother Nature were preparing to sleep. Even the breeze had stopped, as if it, too, needed its slumber. He took in a deep breath of fresh country air. Yes, indeed, Prospect had its good points. He had no doubt that investment money would transform Carson Inn into a vacationer's dream.

Skye and Ali were in the kitchen cleaning up after the evening meal. Fish, of course. The three of them had put a major dent in the afternoon's catch. He'd offered to help with the dishes, but Skye insisted he'd only be in the way and shooed him off.

In truth, she'd been a bit remote since their return from the lake. They'd walked back to the inn hand in hand, but the moment they'd entered the front door, she began moving away from him, physically and emotionally. Her quick change made him mighty uneasy.

Could be that she was attempting a show of indifference for Ali's sake. He understood Skye's concern for her sister. But damn, Ali was a bright girl and intuitive enough, if not downright gifted in some sort of unexplainable way, to see how Skye and he felt about each other. More than once Mac had noticed the approving glance Ali had given them when she'd seen them together. He doubted anything stayed hidden from her view very long.

He heard Skye and Ali talking, the sounds of Ali's chatter growing louder as the two of them neared the screen door. Then Skye poked her head out.

"Coffee's ready," she announced. "I've got some pound cake if you'd like dessert?"

Mac patted his stomach. "No room. Not after that meal you fed me."

That earned her smile. "Would you like your coffee out here?"

"If you'll join me?"

She glanced back in the house, then to the beckoning sunset. "I have to help Ali with homework, but I've got a few minutes." She disappeared behind the door but promptly returned with two steaming cups.

"It's a beautiful night," Mac said as he moved to the edge of the two-seater to make room for her to sit next to him.

Skye stared at the space Mac made for her, enough room to sit but not an inch to spare between them. She couldn't be that close to him, not with Ali about the place and liable to pop outside any moment. The effort to quell her sister's fantastic expectations about her and Mac had been futile so far, and Skye didn't need to give her inspiration for additional wishful thinking.

She stepped back to the railing circling the porch and sat on it, taking note of the flicker of disappointment she saw in Mac's eyes. Sitting quietly, Skye angled her body, letting her back rest against a column, so she could view the lit-up sky. Mac was in her peripheral vision, so his image was vague, but she didn't need to see him clearly to know he was staring at her. She sipped her coffee and grew more uncomfortable by the moment under his scrutiny. She'd made a fool of herself this afternoon. It was so unlike her to let go like that, and she'd never intended to inflict her problems on Mac. What must he think of her?

"About this afternoon," she began weakly. "I don't usually behave so badly. I'm sorry."

"You have nothing to be sorry for."

"Yes, I do."

"That's ridiculous."

"So long as you know it won't happen again. I won't burden you with my problems anymore. I shouldn't have done so this afternoon."

Mac started at her formal words and oh-so-courteous tone. "I was glad to listen, happy you felt comfortable enough to open up with me."

She'd certainly done that, all right, and as much as she'd needed the strength and comfort of his arms, knew better than to let Mac get too close. It would only make losing him all the harder. "Well, thank you for listening," she said cordially, then took several sips from her cup, wanting to end this conversation, which could do nothing but get more intimate by the moment.

Mac set his empty cup on the small iron table beside the swing. Stuffing his hands in his pockets, he took up a standing position next to Skye and eyed the horizon, which was rapidly being taken over by shades of gray.

The lady was an enigma. Sometimes he felt so close to her, certain Skye's response to him was genuine and developing into something very big and very lasting. Then there were the other times, like now, when her aloofness drove him crazy, made him wonder if she would ever truly open up to him. Her coolness hurt like hell, and he sure didn't understand her need to apologize for confiding in him when he wanted to know everything there was to know about the lady.

But there was nothing to be gained by arguing the point. One look in her direction told him that. He recognized the distant look in her eyes, and knew she'd walk off before saying another word about a subject she considered closed, so he channeled his thoughts elsewhere.

"Those baked fish were mighty tasty," he began.

"They were good."

"That lake of yours is bursting with fish. This place would be brimming with fishermen if word got out," he speculated.

"As it is, only the locals use Prospect Lake," she told him.

"So I gather." He had heard a couple of men talk about the fish they'd caught in that lake a day or two ago. "Do you charge fees?"

Skye's eyes narrowed. "Of course not," she said with some irritation. "I wouldn't charge neighbors."

"Just asking," he assured her, and she relaxed. "I can picture cabins along the north shore, a couple of dozen maybe. Bet that would attract people. You could put in a sandy beach and rope off a swimming area. Maybe encourage small boating."

Skye eyed Mac in awe, surprised at his suggestions and the thought that went into making them. His interest pleased her more than she cared to admit. Of course, he hadn't mentioned anything she hadn't already considered, but those kinds of improvements required money. Something in short supply of late. Still, she pondered the ideas.

"Lots of advertising would have to be done," she told him. "We're so far out of the way."

"Yes," he agreed. "And you'd take advantage of the remoteness in your ad campaign. Bill the place as a quiet haven."

"Oh, but I'd also want to provide something other than activities for the outdoorsman."

"Umm, like some entertainment on weekends."

"Exactly!" Her enthusiasm mounted. "A live band, dancing. Of course, I'd want to renovate the inn, preserve the original structure, but add on to accommodate more people and possibly build on a large dining room, complete with a dance floor."

"You could erect a stable—"

"We'd have riding horses," Skye interrupted, something she hadn't thought about, but considered a good idea.

"You already have the store set up for quick purchases, but you might think about adding fishing gear and bait."

"Naturally. And souvenirs," she added.

"You'd turn a tidy profit."

"I think so." But—she exhaled deeply, her shoulders drooped a little—there was always a *but*.

Sensing the change in Skye, Mac asked, "What's going on in that lovely head of yours?"

Her smile was thin as she looked at him. "For the moment, all this talk and planning is speculation, nothing more."

Mac gently stroked Skye's upper arm. "It's none of my business," he began tentatively, "but when you asked for that loan from Milo Craft, did you figure in enough to cover the expansion?''

She answered, ''Yes,'' but her response was hesitant.

''You're worried that he won't come through for you,'' Mac stated.

She shouldn't discuss any of this with Mac. The inn wasn't his business or his concern, but after the interest he'd shown and wonderful suggestions he'd made, well . . . what the heck? ''Some,'' she finally answered. ''I gave him a detailed proposal that accounted for expansion. Without going the whole nine yards with this place, there's little point in going on at all. We'll keep backsliding unless we draw more people.'' Surely Milo would recognize the merit of her plans. And it wasn't as though she were asking for a handout. Her proposal included a payback with hefty interest on his money. Milo would recognize a good deal when he saw one. Wouldn't he?

''I'm sure you're right about the need for expansion,'' Mac was saying.

''Expansion, yes,'' she repeated, but her words were hollow, her stare remote.

''There may be other ways to finance the project if Craft doesn't give you the loan,'' Mac offered, wondering if the time was right to confide his financial situation.

Skye pushed off the railing and crossed her arms in front of her. ''No bank is going to give me a loan, even a small one. I've already been that route.''

''I wasn't thinking about banks.''

Her eyes widened with curiosity when she looked up at him. ''I don't know any other people with that kind of money,'' she said. ''Not personally, anyway.''

''Well now, maybe you do.''

''What are you talking about?'' Skye didn't need this

confusion. What was Mac implying, and why wasn't he answering her instead of standing in front of her looking like the cat who'd swallowed the canary and had been caught in the act? "If you think someone in this town has a stash hidden away in a mattress or buried in some basement, I assure you, you're wrong."

Mac felt a definite tremble in his legs, and his stomach was doing somersaults. He'd never been this nervous. Maybe he should blurt the whole thing out. *Skye, I have money, lots of it. Fact is, I'm loaded. I could give you the money you need twenty times over and never know it was gone.*

"Well?" Chin jutting out, brows knit together, she waited for his response.

"I didn't mean someone here in Prospect." He swiped at his damp brow. "Not exactly, anyway."

"Makes no difference whether we're talking about Prospect, or Oklahoma City, or New York, or the whole of the world. I still don't know anyone with the kind of money Milo has, and I don't understand why you think I do."

"Can we sit down?" Mac took her arm and led her toward the swing. "I want to talk to you about . . . something."

"More riddles, no doubt," she said, but sat down.

He settled beside her. When their eyes met, he took her hand in his large one and gave it a squeeze. "Sometimes it's hard to say certain things," he began, "difficult to find the right words so the other person will understand."

A confused look cut across her features. "What are you trying to tell me?"

"I'm positive you'll get the money you need."

Suddenly her gaze was tender. "That's sweet of you to think so."

Sweet? "No," he said on a shake of his head. "I mean I know it will work out, I'm positive. And do you know what makes me so certain?"

"Because you care about what happens to me and Ali?" she asked hopefully.

"No," Mac retorted quickly, too quickly. "I mean I do care," he corrected before the flash of hurt in her eyes became permanent. "But that's not the reason. It's because . . . because . . . ."

At that moment the screen door opened and Ali stood half-in, half-out the doorway. "I'm ready for you to look over my math," she announced.

Skye quickly pulled her hand from Mac's and bolted up. "Coming."

Mac looked up at her. "We need to talk."

"At the moment I have to help Ali."

"Later, then?"

"I know you mean well, Mac, and I appreciate your concern. You'll never know how much, but there's really nothing more to be said. The only thing to do is wait out Milo's decision." She turned and went into the house.

Skye stepped from her dimly lit bedroom. Barefoot, she made no sound as she moved through the hall. The open expanse of the lobby was cast in midnight shadows, the only light coming from a low-wattage bulb on the wall behind the check-in counter. She hesitated at the foot of the stairs, with trembling fingers tugged at the belt holding her silky, pale blue robe in place.

Before he went to his room for the night, Mac whispered his question in her ear. "Will I see you later?"

She hadn't answered.

Long before his question, Skye knew she wanted to be with him through the night, longed for his touch once more, and since then, thought of little else except the way his body molded so perfectly to hers. She also knew how much she disliked sneaking around in the dark to be with him, but she had to keep this part of their relationship clandestine. Ali would never understand.

Skye swallowed a dry lump forming in her throat. Much as she tried to distance the inner part of herself from Mac, he'd managed to lay open all her fears about the future of the inn, and each day the bond between them grew as quickly as the sunflowers at the edge of the backyard. Sprouting from seeds, the plants reached heights to ten feet within one season. But the leafy stalks disappeared faster than they came. The first sign of cold weather and they turned brown and lifeless. As long as she remembered the sunflowers, she'd be all right.

Skye took the stairs slowly but surely. A light shimmered under Mac's door. She tapped twice lightly and didn't have to wait long before he stood facing her in the open doorway. Her breath caught at the expanse of his naked chest.

He motioned her inside. Skye got no farther than two feet in his room before he pulled her into his arms. His breath was hot, his body charged. His mouth covered hers in a needy, smothering kiss.

"I wasn't sure you'd come," he confessed once he let her go and was closing the door.

"I wasn't either," she told him, thinking what an understatement that was. All evening her heart and head had battled over the decision. "But here I am."

Skye fell into the hardness of his chest once again, taking in the fresh scent of his recently scrubbed skin. She ran her hand down the length of his arms, her fingers on fire as they glided over the muscled contours. She went all hot and liquid inside when his lips trailed kisses down the length of her throat, then down and down, parting the opening of her robe, while his hands deftly loosened the garment from her body.

Mac cupped Skye's breasts in the palms of his hands. Stroking the taut nubs with his thumbs, he nuzzled his face against their fullness. When she moaned in pleasure, he thought he might explode from wanting her. But he wanted to take his time. Much as he ached to be inside her, he longed to know every inch of her body, discover all her secret places. And he wanted to give her pleasure so excruciating that she'd want him as much as he wanted her.

On bended knee, he dotted her torso with kisses, stopping to nibble here and there, savoring the taste of her skin. His hands squeezed her buttocks, pinning her in place as she squirmed in delight while his tongue slid below the narrowness of her waist and still farther until reaching the coiled golden curls that crowned her womanhood.

"Mac." His name came out in a raspy whimper. "You don't know what you're doing to me."

Her hands played in his hair, tugged at his shoulders, but he ignored her demands. His chin nudged her thighs until they opened to him, and his tongue performed a lazy search of her soft mound, gradually coming to stop at her crimson nub. He alternated with strokes and nibbles. Her hips gyrated uncontrollably with each movement of his mouth. Her squeals were ambrosia, fueling his own desire.

"Mac, please, I can't take much more," she begged.

He rose and lifted her from the floor. Although the room was dimly lit, he easily saw the glazed look of longing in her eyes when he gently deposited her on the bed. Standing over her, he unzipped his jeans; his sex, hard and throbbing, plopped out of the confining garment.

He heard her gasp. "I never knew a man could be so beautiful," she murmured, then reached for him. His organ pulsated under her touch, and he knew he was a goner.

Mac lowered himself onto her. She welcomed him with spread legs, and he slid into her warmth easily. He felt so hard, it hurt, and she was wet and slick and ready.

She came quickly. He knew the exact moment her body let go. Another push and he shared her ecstasy. He lay on her for several minutes and felt her breath against his neck.

God, he loved this woman.

The silent admission had been spontaneous and a surprise. He shifted his weight until he settled beside her and let his eyes drift over the contours of Skye's body.

Her smile spoke of contentment when she looked back at him, and Mac knew he could never be without her.

"My Skye," he said out loud before knowing it.

She stirred and eyed him curiously.

"That's how I feel," he explained. Was her lower lip quivering in delight or was it for some other reason? "I love you, Skye."

Her gaze darkened and she fairly jumped from the bed. Mac's chest tightened even as his heart pounded heavy beneath his ribs. He watched her in astonishment while she collected her robe from the floor and awkwardly slipped her arms in the sleeves. What had he done to make her respond this way? "Skye?"

"I'd better get back to my room," she said with her back to him.

When he sat up and reached for her, she stepped

away. "What's wrong? Have I done something? You couldn't be acting this way because I said I—"

She turned suddenly, and he read fear in her startled gaze. "I might fall asleep," she explained shakily. "I want to leave before that happens."

"We need to talk," Mac objected. "There are things I want to tell you."

As if she hadn't heard him, Skye flashed a tight smile before she walked out, but it was the fright in her eyes that scared him.

TEN

"What's the deal?" Ali pushed her half-eaten breakfast plate aside, elbowed the table, and suspiciously eyed both Mac and Skye.

"I don't know what you're talking about," Skye answered in a forced even tone, a futile effort at combating the obvious tension between herself and Mac. "But I do know you ought to eat more than you have. You need lots of energy for taking that big test today."

"Did you two have a fight?" Ali persisted, her gaze shifting back and forth between them. "A lovers' spat?" she added in jest, and chuckled, her mouth twisting into a smirk as her right hand covered her heart in a satirical tragic gesture.

"No, we didn't have a fight," Skye rebutted, without addressing the rest of her sister's comment about lovers, knowing Ali was merely projecting her youthful wishes and couldn't know anything about what had been going on between her and Mac. After all, she'd been careful to exhibit no more than polite friendliness toward him in Ali's presence.

149

"Then how come you're not talking and keep looking at each other like you're both dying to yell or something?"

"No such thing!" Skye protested.

Mac set his fork on his empty plate and rose from the table. "Your sister's right," he said to Ali. "There's nothing going on here except in your imagination." Heading for the kitchen, he stopped to pat Ali's recently brushed hair. "If I've been quiet, it's because I didn't sleep well last night and I've been thinking about all the work ahead of me today."

"But—"

Halfway through the door, he turned back to her. "What's your opinion? Should I use up the last of the paint we bought for the porch and touch up the outside trim or should I start refinishing the upstairs window-sills?"

"Gee, I don't know."

"I'd like to paint," he continued, drawing her thoughts more and more to what he was saying and away from her query of moments ago, "but I hear the weather might turn bad. Think it's going to rain, Ali?"

She shrugged. "Maybe."

"What do you think, Skye?"

She gave him a sideways glance. "I didn't know you were thinking about redoing the sills," she said, grateful he'd managed to change the conversation.

"Some are in rugged shape. The stain on half of them is worn through, and a few are badly dried and splintered from the sun."

"But we don't have a sander," Skye objected, relieved to talk to him about anything. It didn't much matter what. He hadn't said more than two words to her all morning, and she'd returned the silence. "It broke a long time ago."

"Oh, I've got one," he said, his eyes twinkling. Mac extended an arm and made a muscle. "Good, old-fashioned elbow grease."

Ali covered a small laugh with her hand while Skye contained a groan as she watched sinew ripple and pulse against the blue cotton of Mac's shirt.

"The job will take forever," she said.

"No, not quite that long." His mouth slid into a simmering smile, sending shivers up her spine. "And I've got time." The green of his eyes darkened for an instant as his gaze pinned hers. "Patience, too," he added. "Lots of patience."

Skye dropped into the desk chair behind the counter in the lobby. She'd spent the bulk of the morning in the store restocking shelves and taking care of customers who came in at such a steady pace, she'd been unable to leave for more than a few minutes at a time. Setting a combination of checks and bills on the desk, she counted. The little store had brought in eighty-eight dollars, a good morning thanks to a busload of elementary school children and their teachers who'd stopped for refreshments en route to a nature outing.

Correction. Skye set aside a check for $7.59, given to her by Ben Parker. The draft was drawn on a savings and loan that had failed two or three years ago and was about as cashable as the pink and blue play bills in Ali's real estate game. The Parker farm a few miles south of Prospect hadn't done well for the last two seasons, and Skye, along with everyone for miles around, was well aware of Ben's financial woes. Having no cash, he'd given her the check as an IOU. "Makes it more official," he'd told her. She'd given him credit before, and always he insisted on writing a check on the defunct account, paying her what he could, when he could. She had no doubt that as long as Ben Parker drew breath, he'd whittle away at his debt until paying it off. Some people were just that way: true to their word.

Skye placed the paper money in the cashbox, and checks, excluding Ben's, in an envelope for deposit at the bank. Ben's draft went on top of a tidy stack of similar issues in the drawer. The world would be so much less complicated if everyone were as honor-bound as Ben Parker, she speculated, her mind drawing an immediate comparison between him and Henry Walker, who had taken a marriage vow, but broken it as easily as the promise he'd made her mother to do the best he could at managing Carson Inn.

Mac, too, had made a promise. At least to Skye, a vow of love was a trust of honor, and he'd said he loved her. His admission had shaken her, and she'd been off balance ever since. Skye rubbed her tired eyes, their stinging a reminder of the fitful sleep she'd suffered last night. Did he mean those words? she wondered for the umpteenth time since he'd said them the night before. Or had he been merely overcome by the passion of the moment?

He couldn't have fallen in love with her? She'd never wanted that.

That wasn't true.

Her shoulders dropped as she pushed farther down in the chair. Be honest; you wanted Mac to love you. But she'd never actually expected him to, or believed he would. If he did, though, she couldn't imagine his feelings lasting forever. Like her stepfather, he'd eventually become bored with a small, never-changing place like Prospect, and with her, too. Even if Mac Morgan thought he loved her now—and she wasn't entirely convinced he hadn't said the same words to other gullible women who found themselves in his bed—a lasting relationship with a man like him wasn't possible. And she wasn't prepared to go through her days wondering if each new dawn was the one she'd find him gone.

Leave. Mac was bound to go sooner or later. Leave. The word repeated in her mind. Even as every fiber of her being tightened and ached at the thought, she knew she had to make him go sooner. Now. Before she was incapable of pushing him away. Before she turned into a victim, like her mother, imprisoned by love.

Her agreement with Mac was a few days work for room and board. By Skye's count, the bargain they'd struck had been fulfilled a day or two ago. And Ali? Well, she had to understand the time had come for Mac to leave.

She'd thought she could handle a temporary relationship with him, a fling, but she simply wasn't made that way. How arrogant she'd been to be so certain she could keep her emotions in check. She sniffled and dabbed at the liquid pooling in her eyes. She knew what she had to do.

Mac stood and stretched, simultaneously flexing his fingers and arms in an effort to work out a cramp. He'd sanded four windowsills down to their natural wood in two hours. Pain jabbed his wrist, then ran the length of his arm, and a dull ache pounded in his lower back, proof of the frantic rate he'd worked, his bent body utilizing moves and muscles in an unaccustomed manner.

Peering through the window, he watched the swiftly changing sky. The sun shone overhead, but a massive charcoal gray cloud bank was rolling in quickly from the west. The broad sycamore and holly oak bushes in the yard below bent with the increasing wind. Rain wasn't far behind.

He wondered what Skye was doing at this moment. The noon hour was a few minutes away, and he pictured her in the kitchen fixing lunch for them as she'd done every day since his arrival.

But today was different. She'd spoken to him briefly at breakfast, more a show of politeness because Ali had been present, he figured, since she'd said nothing else to him before or since. He'd seen the busload of children pull up the drive and had gone down to the store and offered his help, but she'd dismissed him, insisting she could handle things by herself. He'd gotten the feeling she was referring to more than the two dozen kids who had descended on her.

What had he done to earn her wrath? All morning he'd been trying to figure her mood and the cause of the cold shoulder she'd been giving him. Worry over the inn had to be taking a toll on her emotions, he rationalized, but deep down he knew there was more to the sudden chill between them than concerns about money. Face it, he told himself, Skye's attitude toward him shifted from steamy to icy the minute he'd said he loved her.

He'd moved too fast. She wasn't prepared for his declaration. Hell, even he'd been surprised by his words of love, but the minute he'd spoken them, he knew how right they were, how much he'd meant them.

Mac went to wash up, all the while hoping to find Skye in a better frame of mind when he went downstairs. Maybe all she'd needed was a little time to digest what he'd said and appraise her own feelings. He splashed cold water on his face. A cool spike drove into his spine, but the cause wasn't the ice-cube temperature of the water. It was the sudden realization that Skye might not love him in return.

He'd sensed her reserve, felt she held back some part

of herself. Even when they made love, he felt a barrier between them. He couldn't see it, smell it, or taste it, but the invisible obstacle was there, and he hadn't yet found a way to penetrate the blasted thing, but had assumed one day he would. If Skye didn't love him? That would account for everything.

His stomach growled, but hunger vanished, replaced by sour bile that churned in his belly.

She might not love him.

That frightening speculation choked out every other thought until his temples throbbed.

She felt something for him, he reassured himself. He couldn't be wrong about that. Innately he knew Skye wasn't the kind of woman to bed a man on a whim. Pushing back every thought but that one, he went to the kitchen.

The large, square room was empty when he entered. Experience told him Skye wasn't in the store at this hour. He went to the window over the sink and searched the backyard, now under a veil of dark shadows from the overhead clouds. Determining that she wasn't outside, he turned in to the room, leaned against the counter, and ruefully eyed the refrigerator. He definitely wasn't in the mood to eat.

About to search for Skye, he strode to the door, stopping when he spotted her walking toward him.

"I didn't hear you come down." She swept past him and drew a loaf of bread from the box on the counter. "I'll get you some lunch."

"You're going to join me?"

"I've eaten."

He stared at the back of her head. Her hair was knotted up, although several strands had broken their confinement and danced about her back and shoulders.

He stifled the urge to taste the skin at the base of her neck.

They'd always lunched together, he silently complained in self-pity. Her tone may have sounded normal when she spoke, but her behavior wasn't status quo at all. Mac gritted his teeth and watched her move about the kitchen.

She set a sandwich on the table, then poured steaming soup in a bowl. He took a seat in front of the offering but didn't eat.

"Storm's coming in quickly," he said for lack of knowing what else to say.

Standing at the sink with her back to him, she lifted her head, and although he couldn't see her features, he knew she was studying the sky through the window. "Weather reports say we're in for some wind with this one," she commented. "Is the work shed locked?" She still hadn't looked at him. Not once.

"Bolted the door and windows last night."

She nodded.

"Want me to head into Lindsay in a couple of hours and pick up Ali rather than have her on that bus in a storm?"

"It's supposed to be a fast-moving front," she said, "and will probably be over by the time school lets out. If not, the school will postpone the run and keep the kids there."

Mac went to the refrigerator and grabbed a beer. "Want one?"

"No."

"Fine with me," he said irritably, and went back to the table, where he pushed his dish aside. Uncapping the bottle, he downed half the brew in big gulps.

"You're not eating?"

"I'm not hungry either," he returned so sharply that

she drew back, but was looking at him now. Wide-eyed, her stare was full of question and something else. It was the something else that made his breath catch while he waited to hear whatever she was bound to say. A rumble in his gut told him he wasn't going to like it.

"We have to talk," she finally told him.

"I couldn't agree more." At that, Mac rose and pulled out a chair for Skye.

"I'd rather stand."

"Then we'll both stand." He pushed the chair back under the table and stepped toward her, hating the drawn look of her features and the tension in the air, so thick he didn't even notice the first fat splats of rain that plopped noisily on the porch outside.

She shot him an I-give-up kind of glance and took a seat at the table. He followed suit. God, he longed to take Skye in his arms, dispel whatever fears she had, banish every doubt from her mind and heart.

A new fear suddenly gripped him. Had she learned his true identity before he'd had a chance to tell her himself? If so, that would explain her coolness. He'd rather she'd gotten mad and yelled obscenities at him. The silent treatment was driving him crazy.

"We've got to clear the air," he announced.

"Yes."

"I'm not the person you think, and I'm sorry. But, Skye, you have to understand—"

"You're exactly the man I thought you were," she interrupted.

"I am?"

"Of course," she answered matter-of-factly.

"But I've said things." He swallowed the dry wad in his throat. "And I've done things I shouldn't. Damn." He drank the last of his beer. "This is hard."

Skye stiffened as Mac spoke, and she thought she was going to be sick. So he regretted his words of love after all. That was for the best, she tried telling herself. Better now than later. She wished her heart held the belief as strongly as her head. Never mind. She couldn't give in to her emotions now. Much as she wanted to cry, she had to finish what she'd started. There was no postponing the inevitable any longer. She'd made up her mind to tell Mac he had to go, and that's what she was going to do.

"I'm sorry if I hurt you," he said with so much tenderness, Skye barely managed to keep from going to him, throwing her arms around him, and begging for his love.

"I never meant to do that," he continued.

"You haven't hurt me," she said truthfully. She was wounded, all right, but Mac wasn't responsible. She couldn't blame him for her pain when she'd known exactly what she was getting into and had charged ahead anyway.

Mac hoped she was speaking the truth, but if Skye wasn't hurt by his deception, then what exactly was the cause of the strain between them? Maybe she didn't know anything about the act he'd been playing after all. He shifted uneasily in his chair, his confusion growing by the moment.

"Who do you think I am?" he asked.

Her gaze was puzzled when meeting his. "I don't understand."

"You said you know who I am, so tell me."

She studied him for a few seconds, and he thought she might not answer him, but then she said, "I've no delusions about you, Mac. You're the man who showed up on my doorstep with little cash in his pockets, no job, and no roof over his head."

"Oh."

"Is there something else I should know?" Pursing her lips together, she shook her head. "I take that back. I don't want or need to know more."

Skye hadn't discovered his deception. Something else was responsible for the trouble between them. He stifled the urge to come clean about himself right then and there. First things first. At the moment he had to learn what was troubling her so he could fix it.

"Skye, what's going on? Please tell me." Getting no response, he continued. "You've got to talk to me."

"As you said, it's hard."

His hand reached across the table for hers, but she pulled away at his first touch. "I also said I'm a patient man. If you can't talk to me about whatever is bothering you right now, I'll wait until you can. But, Skye, you have to tell me sooner or later."

How well she knew. At the moment, however, she couldn't bear to look one more second into eyes that gazed back at her so lovingly and full of understanding. She abruptly rose and stood in front of the sink with her back to him. The rain came down fast, driven at a forty-five-degree angle by a fierce wind. She closed her eyes to the weather and wrapped herself with her arms. "I do have something to tell you," she said in a voice that sounded as if it belonged to someone else.

"Go on."

She felt his presence when he stepped behind her. "I want you to leave."

ELEVEN

"Leave?" Mac repeated, stunned.

"Yes. Right away."

"But why? What have I done?"

Skye turned in his direction. Her face, drained of color, was long and serious. "You've done nothing," she insisted. "I'm worried that Ali is getting too fond of you, that's all."

Mac took a step toward her, but stopped when Skye drew up rigid before him. He was very afraid she really meant for him to go. "Your sister doesn't know anything about . . . about us," he choked out. "And would it be so terrible if she did?"

"You know it would."

Troubled, Mac rubbed his temple. "There's got to be more to it than concern for Ali."

The corner of her mouth lifted in a sarcastic smile. "We've had our fun," she told him caustically. "It's been great. But it's over and time for you to move on. Don't make more out of it than that."

Oh, he'd make more of it, all right. How could he

not? It two quick strides Mac narrowed the space between them and pulled her to him. Her breath escaped in a rush against his chest. Her hands came up and pushed against his shoulders, but he pinned her in place and lifted her chin until her gaze met his. She stopped struggling, but when she looked at him, her blue eyes were a mix of anger, despair, and determination.

"Let me go," she ordered.

He felt her heartbeat against his, its rhythm quick as his own. "I will," he said, "but not before you see why it's impossible for me to leave."

As though to stave off his advances, her eyelids clamped shut as his mouth descended on hers, but she didn't try to get away. His kiss was urgent and hungry. He had to make her see that she couldn't simply discharge him and expect him to oblige without a fight.

He heard her whimper and sensed the battle waging inside her. She wanted to return his kiss, not just stand there taking it like some heroic captive who had no choice but to endure his advances. Then she moaned, and at the same instant the tension in her body broke and she was kissing him back, her arms tightening around him.

Hands groping, exploring, he held her for a long time, his lips never leaving hers. Leave Skye? Impossible. Now she had to know that, too.

Skye took in a deep breath when his lips finally pulled away from hers, and rested her head against the heavy beating of his heart. The sultry, warm air of the closed-up kitchen, mingled with Mac's scent of pure masculinity, filled her lungs. She was suddenly aware of the trampling sounds of rain driven against the house by the wind.

She hadn't meant to return his kiss. The idea had been to prove that she was impervious to his charms.

Ha! As if it were possible to act the part of a mannequin in his arms. The fact that she had so little control over her reactions as far as Mac was concerned only strengthened her determination to make him leave before she found herself powerless even to ask.

"There." Mac set her a couple of feet from him. His eyelids were heavy with emotion, his grin both tender and confident. "Now ask me to leave," he dared.

"I have to do just that," Skye managed in spite of the fact that her throat had turned to gravel.

Mac went cold as if he'd been suddenly drained of all his blood. "You don't mean it."

"Yes, I do."

Dumbfounded, he began, "But I thought—"

"What?" Skye interrupted. "That one kiss would change my mind?"

"Yes, I did," he said in a low rumble.

Courage, Skye silently commanded. She had to find some. Pulling herself up erect, she met his eyes and refused to let herself avoid his confused and hurt gaze. "You'd leave sooner or later," she said. "Might as well be today instead of three days from now or next week or whenever you take it into your head to go."

"You're frightened," he charged. "That's it, isn't it?" Mac paced a few steps in one direction, then back again, cutting a path in front of Skye, his mind digesting the possibility he'd voiced. "Of course, that's it," he said on a shake of his head, then stopped and turned back to her. "I said I love you, and it scares you to death."

"I'm not afraid," she said shakily.

"What's got you scared?" He stepped slowly toward her. "Is it me? Are you afraid of me, Skye? I love you. Do you think I didn't mean it? Well, I've got news for you, lady. I don't use words like that lightly. I meant it then and I mean it now. Mac Morgan loves Skylar Carson. Should I carve out a heart with our names in the old oak tree? Will that make you believe me?''

Skye halted his forward movement with her upturned hand. "I believe you, but . . .''

"But what?" When she didn't answer immediately, Mac added, "Have I got it all wrong? Maybe you don't feel the same way about me, and that's why you want me to go?" He searched her features, desperate for a clue. "Have I moved too quickly for you?"

Skye clasped her hands in front of her. She had to gain control. This wasn't working out at all as she'd planned. Clearing her throat, she said, "You don't understand."

He threw his hands in the air. "Ha, a revelation! You bet I don't." His tone was charged with irritation, his anger deepening by the second. "You tell me to leave, give me reasons that make no sense at all, and expect me to trot along like a good little boy. I'm no kid. I'm a man. A man who's held you in his arms, made love to you. And you won't convince me that you didn't want me every bit as much as I wanted you. Can you honestly tell me you don't care at all about me?" He stood directly in front of her, his brooding gaze locking with hers. "Tell me you have no feeling for me," he dared. "If you can do that, I'll leave."

No, she couldn't say that. "I do care about you, Mac," she said, and watched his features soften with her admission. "But we have no future together. I think it best to end things now."

"If I disagree?"

"I'm sorry."

"Just like that. You're sorry."

He glared down at her, his taste for argument still strong. She was desperate to find a way to make him see that she was right, even if it meant being cruel. "No matter how you make me feel when I'm in your arms, you're not the man for me. Never will be." She took a deep breath and continued. "Accept it. We're mismatched, and you'll never have what it takes to satisfy me."

"And what would that be?" His tone was sharp and angry.

"I need a man who can offer more than his body on a cold night. I want security, a future, a man who values these things, too."

"Money," he said abruptly, a high-wattage light switching on in his mind. "You want money." A bolt of lightning flashed in the darkened sky, followed by a thunderous sound that made the floor under his feet rumble.

Skye hadn't thought in precisely those terms, but answered, "Yes, money's a part of it." A goal-oriented person with ambition usually acquired some of the green stuff, she reasoned.

Mac's shoulders sagged on an expelled breath. So that's the way it was; Skye wanted a man with money. *Here I am*, was ready to slide off his tongue. *I've got more money than a hundred people could spend in a lifetime.* But he couldn't tell her. Not when all along he had assumed she valued him for who he was, not the balance in his checkbook.

He pictured Skye eagerly submitting to his embrace once she understood the nature of his finances, and it took every ounce of his willpower to keep from blurting out the truth to her.

Much as he wanted her in his arms at that moment and by his side always, he couldn't live his life wondering if the woman he loved was with him because of his money and would walk out on him the day he had none.

He ought to comply with Skye's request, and leave. She'd made her feelings clear. But even as he thought to go, Mac knew he couldn't do it. Money might be important to Skye, but he didn't believe there weren't other things she valued as much. More. His mind drifted to the nights spent together in his bed. No matter how she denied her feelings, he couldn't have misunderstood the satisfied glow in her cheeks or the genuine caring he saw in her gaze after they made love.

"You don't have to leave right this minute," Skye said, dragging his attention and pained heart back to the present. "What with the storm and all. But I'd appreciate it if you would leave in the morning."

"Morning, sure," he returned, all the while thinking he wasn't ready to give up on Skye. He could convince her that love was enough. He had to.

Where would Mac go? That question troubled Skye all through the afternoon. She stood on the front porch, her gaze aimlessly drifting. The rain had stopped. Roaring wind had quieted to a whimper of a breeze, and the late afternoon sun attempted an appearance. The air was dewy and drenched with fresh scents left by the storm. Up the road, activity was once again evident as people began to come out of houses and stores. Old Mrs. Garver, followed by a parade of her strays, cut a jagged path across Main Street, stopping here and there to talk to or pet one or another of the cats. Ali would be home any minute. The storm had ended before causing any delay in her departure from school.

Where would Mac go once he left Prospect? She shouldn't be concerned about his next address, not when he was obviously skilled at making the best of any situation. Although he'd appeared angry and disappointed when she insisted he leave, he'd probably regrouped by now, put their relationship in perspective, and was looking forward to seeing new places and meeting new people. Her heart skipped a beat. Would there be a new woman in his life, too?

More than once she'd had to stop herself from going to him, telling him she'd made a mistake, admitting she didn't want him to leave. Mac was upstairs. He'd been there since they talked. Once, while standing at the top landing, she heard the scraping of sandpaper against wood, the sounds drifting from a guest room near the end of the long hall. She'd been surprised he'd gone back to work when she hadn't managed anything productive, physically or mentally.

Skye hurt. She ached all over, from a dull drumming in her head to crampy knots in her stomach. Her monthly period, a few days off, was responsible for the sick feeling, she tried to convince herself, in spite of the fact that she rarely had such symptoms during her cycle. She rubbed her arms, fighting off a chill. Who was she kidding? Certainly not herself. There was but one cause for her misery, and his name was Mac Morgan.

In consolation, she reminded herself that the hurt she was experiencing was nothing in comparison to the pain she'd feel if she got used to having Mac around, then he left.

A rumbling sound up the street captured Skye's attention. She spotted the old yellow school bus coming to a stop.

Ali skipped from the last step and waved. "Hi," she called out to Skye.

"How'd your test go?" Skye asked when Ali climbed the porch stairs.

Ali's nose scrunched up. "All right, I guess."

"Don't tell me it was that bad?"

"Okay, I won't." She clamped her mouth shut and stared at Skye with a challenging gaze.

"Maybe you'd better."

"I might have passed," Ali said optimistically. "It was so hard, and I'm not sure."

"Let's hope for the best," Skye offered as they made their way inside.

Ali dropped her books on the counter and headed for the kitchen, with Skye following. "Where's Mac?" she asked, scanning the room.

"Working upstairs."

"Sanding?"

"Ummm."

"Good thing he decided to do that instead of paint." She took a pitcher of orange juice from the refrigerator and poured a tall glass. "Did you see the way that rain came down? For a while I thought I was going to get stranded at school. Yuk!" She downed the juice in big gulps.

"There are worse things," Skye teased, and searched the contents of a cupboard for something quick and easy for supper. "What do you feel like eating tonight?"

"Whatever."

Whatever, indeed. Skye wished she'd taken something from the freezer earlier, but she had been too preoccupied. As it was, she hadn't a clue what to make. "I'd better do some shopping," she thought out loud, eyeing the sparse contents of the cabinet.

"Can we go into Lindsay?" Ali asked excitedly. "All the kids say that new place makes great fries and onion rings. Please, Skye. We haven't gone anywhere in ages.''

"I don't know, Ali," Skye hedged, mentally tabulating the additional cost to her wallet of eating a meal out, even a cheap one at a fast-food place. Still, Ali had been so good and uncomplaining about the tight budget Skye had enforced on both of them. One glance at her sister's expectant gaze and she decided they needed a break from routine, not to mention that the upbeat atmosphere of a restaurant might provide a perfect setting to tell Ali that Mac was leaving in the morning.

"You can't leave tomorrow," Ali told Mac in a loud voice, causing the man in the booth behind them to turn and stare.

"You knew Mac's stay in Prospect was temporary," Skye reminded, and not for the first time regretted she'd found no polite way to keep Mac from joining them for dinner.

"You have to stay for my birthday," she told Mac, ignoring Skye.

"When's that?" Mac asked.

"This Thursday," she told him, full of hope. "You don't really have to go until after that, do you?"

Thank you, sweetheart. Mac silently expressed his gratitude. He'd been trying to come up with a legitimate reason to stick around for a while longer, and now Ali had provided him with one.

"Another day or two won't hurt anything," he said, not the least bit surprised by the irritated scowl that cut across Skye's features. He grinned mischievously. "Is that okay with big sister?"

A warning alarm went off in Skye's head. What was he doing? "Don't you have someplace to go?" she blurted. "I mean I thought you had to leave tomorrow," she added, in hope of jogging his memory about how adamant she'd been that he go in the morning.

"I'm not in that big of a hurry," he said so casually that she wanted to drench his oh-so-handsome head with her iced tea.

"It's all set then," Ali chirped, and took a bite of her onion burger. "You'll be here for my party."

"We don't want to force Mac to stay if he has other plans," Skye tried one more time.

"But he wants to stay with us," Ali told Skye, then looked to Mac. "Don't you?"

"Sure thing, sweetheart." The glint in his eye was full of challenge when he met Skye's gaze. "Long as it's no imposition?"

Trapped. No doubt about it. All Skye could say was a defeated "Of course not," and that was that. Ali went on to tell Mac about her friends on the guest list and the three-layer German chocolate cake Skye promised to bake for the occasion.

"We'll hang lots of balloons; streamers, too," Mac told Ali, matching her enthusiasm, keeping one vigilant eye on Skye the whole time. Silent and brooding, she sat across the booth from him, taking an occasional nibble of her cheeseburger.

"Not hungry?" he asked her after a while.

She smiled at him through gritted teeth. "I've lost my appetite."

"Too bad. The food here is mighty tasty." He bit into a second plump double-beef-and-cheese hamburger. He'd be tempted to feel sorry for Skye's predicament if he hadn't acted for her own good. Sensing her restraint, he figured it was taking all her willpower to keep from hurling a few choice words at him. After the stunt he'd just pulled, he wouldn't blame her if she did lose control. But his cause was just, he reasoned. The decision to linger awhile longer in Prospect was one he'd made hours before. It was the means he'd been uncertain about until Ali brought up the subject of her birthday.

Meanwhile, Skye could shoot all the disparaging looks at him that she wanted, but he wasn't about to change his mind. He was staying, no matter how the lady protested, which, in his opinion, was way too much for a woman who'd insinuated he'd been little more than a diversion from routine for her.

Skye had to come to know love was enough. Hell, he'd gladly give up his entire fortune if it meant having her. He needed her blind faith, her trust, and most of all, her unqualified love. Somehow he had to make Skye admit her feelings for him ran deeper than a brief affair, and their love was more precious than any possession. He longed for her lifelong pledge of love. He'd make it so . . . somehow.

_____ TWELVE _____

"What a lovely old place," Mrs. Halpern squealed, her laughing eyes roving the lobby. "So quaint."

"Thank you," Skye told her, sensing the woman's comment was meant as a compliment.

"Earl and I—" she gave her husband a fleeting glance of acknowledgment "—hope we'll be living here soon. We're so excited."

Earl Halpern grunted. "Now, dear, don't get your hopes up yet."

"But I'm sure it will work out. Why, look at this place. Isn't it everything we're looking for?" she asked, not really expecting an answer. "The whole town is just like we pictured."

Skye plucked two matching keys from their hook and handed them to her newest guests. "You folks buying a house in Prospect?"

The couple briefly locked gazes, making Skye think she had asked a difficult question.

Clearing his throat, Earl tore away from his wife's stare. "We hope to," he told Skye. "It's all a bit premature, you see.'' He smiled warmly. ''My wife's expectations are already too high.''

The thin woman's silvery hair shimmered in the midday sun drifting in through the front windows. ''Earl is retiring in a month,'' she explained. ''Thirty years with the telephone company in Tulsa.'' Her lined mouth slanted into a proud smile. ''Started out as a lineman and worked himself right up into management. But now we want to get back to our roots. We both grew up in small towns.''

''And do it cheaply,'' her husband added.

Skye was glad to hear about people moving into town for a change, instead of leaving. ''Good luck,'' she told them sincerely. ''There's some good property bargains in Prospect,'' she commented, numerous FOR SALE signs coming to mind.

''So we hear,'' Earl muttered.

Skye turned toward the thumping sounds of Mac's boots on the stairs. She stiffened and couldn't control her sharp intake of air or the sudden tremor in her pulse. Coiled and ready to spring, she felt like a warrior waiting to do battle. They'd spoken little since their outing the night before, and as far as she was concerned, the man had a lot to answer for. Questioning his motives, not to mention the underhanded methods he'd employed for staying on at the inn, had been impossible at breakfast with Ali present. Then he left on a spur-of-the-moment decision to drive Ali to school and keep his promise to view her paintings. When he returned, she'd been busy in the store with a couple of customers, then, behind schedule, rushed to prepare rooms for the Halperns and Donald Loggerson, an insurance salesman who had checked in minutes before.

Mrs. Halpern's high-pitched twang drew Skye's attention. ''I'm something of a history buff and an amateur collector," she was saying, her gaze taking in the overhead twin fixtures that dangled from the high ceiling. Her thin hand clutched her chest and she gasped in surprise. "Don't tell me those are Tiffany?"

"Originals," Skye confirmed. "My grandfather had them railroaded in, but one broke during the trip and had to be reordered. He threw a party once they were finally hung."

"How exciting."

Mac hoisted the Halperns' one piece of luggage from the floor.

"Thank you, young man," the woman said, and followed behind him and her husband, but stopped at the foot of the stairs. "Miss Carson, you won't mind if I have a look around? This is such a fascinating place."

"Feel free." There was a time when the inn, with its one-of-a-kind custom furnishings, was the cultural showcase of the entire region. Now things merely looked old, and only a handful of people recognized the few quality pieces that had weathered time, so Skye was pleased at the woman's request.

Looking satisfied, Mrs. Halpern caught up to her husband and muttered something inaudible in his ear, then waved down to Skye before disappearing up the stairs.

It wasn't long before Mac came down again. Close behind him was the insurance salesman.

Donald Loggerson scratched his unruly dark hair in confusion. "I've seen you somewhere," he was saying to Mac's back. "Are you sure we haven't met?"

"Yes," Mac answered, his gaze fixed in front of him.

The man, a head shorter and a foot wider than Mac, stepped to the counter, but his eyes remained locked on Mac. "I never forget a face," he mused.

"I probably look like someone you know," Mac suggested.

"No, that's not it."

Mac turned from the squat man and leaned into the counter to face Skye. "The windowsills are done, and the stain shouldn't take long to dry. Think I'll get some of that outside painting done."

"We need to talk," she told him sharply.

"I know where I saw you," Loggerman blurted out, his look of recognition instantly shifting to bewilderment. "But it can't be. You cannot be the man I saw on the cover of *Financial Review* last year?"

Frowning in irritation, Mac turned on the man. "If I were on the cover of that magazine, do you think I'd be working as a handyman in Prospect, Oklahoma?"

"N-no." Loggerman's cheeks colored. "Of course, you couldn't be that man."

Mac turned on his heel and headed for the back door. Loggerman shook his head. "Talk about feeling stupid," he told Skye.

"Don't worry about it," she assured him, even though his assumptions amazed her. Some people saw the rich and famous everywhere they looked, she guessed. "I assure you Mac isn't anything like the man you read about," she added, and couldn't refrain from an unspoken wish that he shared a few qualities with the kind of man who was successful. Like having goals and the ambition and tenacity to work hard at achieving them.

She frowned. Mac took one day at a time. All his tomorrows were blank sheets of paper, and that's the way he liked to live his life.

When she looked over the counter at Loggerson, he was eyeing her in bewilderment.

"Mr. Loggerson, is something wrong?"

"No, no," he said quickly, his chubby cheeks flapping with a few brisk shakes of his head. "It's only that you called the handyman Mac?"

"Yes."

"Hmmm."

"What is it?"

"His last name?" Loggerson asked.

Where was this going? Skye wondered, but answered, "Morgan," and waited for some sort of explanation for the man's curious behavior. When none came, she asked, "Does the name mean something to you?"

His gray sport jacket gapped as he stuffed his hands inside his trouser pockets and attempted a casual stance. "I'm sure it's a coincidence." His full shoulders rose, as did his brow. "Has to be."

"What?"

"Well," he said tentatively, his tone lowering an octave, "at the risk of appearing foolish again, that fella on the cover of that magazine, the one I mentioned before. I'd swear his name was Mac, too, but for the life of me, I can't recall the last name. Might have been Morgan."

"Impossible," Skye said vehemently.

"Then again, Michaels sounds right," he said, more to himself than Skye. "Or Miller. That's it. Must have been Miller," he decided.

"Yes, must have been," Skye agreed.

Dusk had stolen the lobby's light. Skye fumbled with the lamp switch until a yellow glow split the shadows of approaching night. Her fingers rapped an anxious beat against the desktop. Mac was avoiding her, and doing a fine job of it, too.

Between catering to guests' needs and to several

neighbors who had come by the store for a loaf of bread or gallon of milk, she'd been too busy to search him out, and he'd been conspicuously avoiding her, not even coming in for lunch at the usual hour. When she had finally gotten a breather in the middle of the afternoon, she located him on a ladder painting the shutters on the east side of the house.

"Mac Morgan, come down here this instant and talk to me," she'd hollered up at him, the intended sternness in her voice tapering off to a pleading request as his muscled thighs and shapely, firm behind filled her gaze.

"Yes, ma'am," he'd called down to her, and, paintbrush in hand, saluted. "Anything you say, boss lady."

She stamped the ground in frustration. "Don't call me that. You don't work here anymore. At least you're not supposed to be," she corrected. "But then, you don't seem to remember that."

Mac took the rungs two at a time until his feet settled on the ground. When he turned, she saw he was grinning at her. What was so funny? Her?

"You're laughing at me," she charged.

"No, I'm not," he denied, but the tremor in his voice said otherwise.

The man was impossible! Feet set apart, hands on hips, Skye squared off for a fight. "Yes, you are," she insisted. "But it makes no difference. No matter what you do or how you try to avoid me, we're going to settle a few things."

Mac's smile broadened. "You're awfully cute when you're all hot and bothered."

Skye took a step back. "I'm no such thing!"

"Sure you are," he said absolutely, and pressed a palm to her forehead. "Skin's way too warm. Clammy, too. Cheeks are flushed, and—'' he paused and winked, ''—you jump like you're on fire when I touch you.''

''I do not,'' Skye instantly rebutted, even knowing his touch had made her start and his hand against her skin had felt like a hot poker.

''Love,'' Mac mused with a faraway look in his eye.

''What are you talking about?''

He met her gaze once more. ''Do you suppose you're in love? That would explain all your symptoms.''

Skye muttered an expletive under her breath. ''You're impossible.''

''Aren't I, though?''

Then Ali's bus had chugged up the road, and Skye had been forced to terminate their conversation. No great sacrifice, given the fact that it wasn't going anywhere, thanks to Mac's double-talk.

''This isn't the end of it,'' she had threatened before leaving him. ''We will talk.''

''I look forward to it,'' he'd called after her.

Skye set her folded hands on top of the desk. Mac couldn't avoid her forever. Soon enough, she'd make him understand that she wanted him to leave, and he had no choice in the matter. No more excuses. No more ploys.

The ringing telephone brought her thoughts back to the present. She picked up to a prospective guest, took a reservation, posted the name in the book, and blocked off the large suite for three nights the following month.

She stared at the reservation for a long time. There was something about ink set to paper that seemed so official and unalterable. But that wasn't so. Things had a way of changing. Even a name in a book was in jeopardy of being lined out. If she didn't come up with the money owed the bank, that's exactly what would happen to the name she'd so decisively written.

Once again she picked up the receiver, this time to dial out. She eyed the desktop calendar while waiting for someone on the other end to pick up. Milo had assured her that he'd contact her when he arrived back from his trip. By all accounts, he should have returned sometime during the day.

She ought to wait for his call, give him a chance to settle in and unwind. No doubt he would get in touch with her soon. But Skye's patience for waiting was gone. Knowing how desperate her situation was becoming, Milo would forgive her impatience, she thought.

His homecoming had been delayed a few days, the maid informed Skye, giving assurances she would inform Mr. Craft of her call as soon as he arrived.

There was nothing to do but go about her routine and hope he'd return her call soon. She collected cash and checks from a pouch in the drawer and made up a deposit ticket, taking heart in the fact that the amount, like the last deposit, was for more money than usual. For a moment she could forget that this money would do little more than temporarily stave off the continual depletion of the Carson Inn account.

Fortunately the unseasonable heat wave broke, allowing Skye to shut down the air-conditioner she'd turned on earlier in the day for guest comfort. She sat up in her bed, surrounded by the darkness of late night, a cool breeze from the open window moving over her body.

She couldn't sleep. Her stomach fluttered mercilessly, and much as she tried, she couldn't stop worrying about the future. Waiting was hell, she decided. But that's all she could do. Wait for Milo's response to her request for a loan, knowing his answer would alter her and Ali's life forever. Wait for Mac to leave.

Wait for life to return to normal, whatever normal was. She wasn't so sure she knew anymore.

And through all the waiting she desperately tried to suppress thoughts of Mac. With him sleeping under her roof, a thirty-second journey from her bedroom door, the effort was futile.

Skye gathered her knees up, folded her arms around them. The harder she tried not to think about him, the more she did think about him. Closing her eyes, she pictured him in his room, his long, strong body stretched out on the bed. Since he slept nude, no clothes would conceal any part of his body from her vision, and she saw herself stepping into his room. Drawing from vivid memory, she imagined every inch of him, and sighed in yearning. He would see her enter, but wouldn't speak. Words were pointless. His gaze, full of longing for her, would say it all. She would go to him, and he'd take her to a place removed from all troubles. In his embrace she would find passion and pleasure, security and serenity. Everything would be right again.

But that wasn't so. Nothing was right, and the security she found in his arms was false. She'd pay dearly if she gave in to her desire; the price extracted would be even greater heartache than she felt now. The best thing was to forget about Mac Morgan. That's what she had to do. But oh, why did it have to be so hard?

In a state of partial undress, Mac eyed the four walls of his bedroom. He could feel them closing in on him. His hands formed tight fists as he crossed the room and stood in front of the window, looking out into the dark night. He despised indecision, something he'd never been guilty of until recently.

He was going mad, and Skye was to blame.

He'd showered and shaved in anticipation of being with her tonight. The chances that she would come to him as she'd done before ranged from mighty slim to nonexistent, so he had planned on going to her instead. But by the time he'd toweled the wetness of a shower from his body and stepped into a pair of jeans, second thoughts undermined his plan. Now, shirtless and shoeless, he worried over possible repercussions of rushing her.

Raking his fingers through his damp hair, he wished for more time with Skye, but had none to spare. An earlier telephone conversation with his assistant, the talk revolving around an unexpected business problem that required Mac's personal attention, confirmed how few the days were before he had to leave. Who was he kidding? He ought to hightail it back to Dallas right this moment, but the prospect of business as usual, without Skye, held no appeal.

Mac shrugged into the first clean shirt he laid his hands on. He was a man of action, he reminded himself as he stepped barefooted into the hall. No matter how hard Skye tried to push him away, he'd bet his fortune she loved him enough to rise above her need for money. He knew she thought of him as a liability, just another mouth to feed, and it hurt like hell. Somehow she had to realize that what they had together, and could have in the future, was worth more than all the riches in the world. And he had to know, beyond a doubt, that Skye's love wasn't purchased with stock options and worldwide bank accounts.

Black filled the narrow space beneath Skye's door, vanquishing Mac's hope that, like him, she couldn't sleep. "What the hell," he muttered under his breath, and knocked anyway, his open hand thumping lightly against the wood so as not to disturb others in the house, most especially Ali.

"Who the . . . ?" Skye mumbled when she heard the muffled rapping at her door. Wearing nothing but bikini panties, she searched the room for a cover-up and located her extra long T-shirt on the chair where she'd left it earlier. One of the guests wanted something or had a complaint, she speculated, her sleep interrupted on more than one occasion by late night requests.

With a sleepy smile, she opened the door. "Can I help . . . you?" Her inquiry trailed when she recognized Mac. He pushed into her room, closing the door behind him, forcing her to step back.

"You wanted to talk," was all he said in explanation for his intrusion.

"Now? You want to talk now?" Her pulse quickened and a warmth spread rapidly from her core to all parts of her body. "This is insane." She ducked behind him and reached for the doorknob. "You're insane. We'll talk, all right, but it'll be in broad daylight."

"You want light?" He found the wall switch that illuminated the entire room.

Skye blinked, as much from the full impact of a freshly bathed and shaven Mac hovering over her as from the sudden brightness. She picked up his scent of soap as he crossed in front of her. "I don't think you're here to talk," she charged.

"I bet you hope not." Even as his tone was husky, his gaze took in the room he'd seen only from the doorway. Before Skye had an opportunity to respond, he turned and said, "Look, we were both busy today, and I feel bad that we didn't get a chance to talk then."

"Of course, it had nothing to do with the way you've been avoiding me?"

He gave her a penitent glance. "I confess. I'm guilty. But I'm here now, and you are, too. It's quiet. We're alone, and no one's going to interrupt." When she shot him a doubtful look, he added, "I'm here to clear the air between us, nothing else." Wrists touching, he held his hands out to her. "Tie me up if you need reassurances that I'll behave."

"Don't tempt me."

"Could I?"

His double meaning didn't escape Skye. "No," she answered sharply, hoping he believed the lie.

Unfazed, Mac settled in one of two matching rose-print chairs tucked in a corner. His gaze was unreadable as he eyed her from across the room. "I can stay or I can leave. It's up to you."

"Stay," she finally said after assessing the situation. What difference did the time or place make? she concluded. Sitting quietly, Mac appeared willing to listen at this moment, something that might easily change by morning. He'd already proven his unpredictability.

Skye moved to take the chair next to his until she saw the hunger in his eyes as his gaze fixed on her bare legs. Stopping short, she went to her closet instead and donned her longest, heaviest terry robe.

"Won't you be hot in that?" he asked when she settled next to him.

"No," she answered, and pulled the belt tighter around her waist, knowing full well she was bound to be warm in any event. Better her rising temperature be caused by thick garments than the swell of heat she felt whenever his eye captured any part of her body.

Mac didn't dispute her word directly, but got his point across when he went to the partially open window and lifted the sash higher. "You won't mind a little more air?" he asked, his tone faintly mocking. "Seeing as how you're dressed for cold weather."

Skye didn't answer. The last thing she wanted was to banter with him when there were important issues to settle. "That was a dirty trick you pulled yesterday. Using my sister that way was despicable," she charged. "What I don't understand is why you did it. You'd planned to leave soon anyway. At least that's what you told me. Several times, as I recall. What possible difference could a couple of days make to you?"

"What do you want me to address first? How despicable I am? Why I want to stay a bit longer? Or shall we talk about your general confusion?"

"Don't toy with me, Mac." Skye pointed an angry finger at him. "First time I saw you, I knew you had no honor, knew you were the kind to take advantage of people."

Anger slammed into his narrowed eyes like a fist. "Exactly who did I take advantage of?"

Skye flinched at his clipped tone but refused to be intimidated. "Me," she said with certainty. "I took you in, fed you, gave you my father's clothes to wear." She pinned him with a stern look of her own. "One thing about you, Mac Morgan. You know a good thing when you see it. That's why you refuse to leave. If you had any self-respect, you wouldn't want to live off other people."

Mac abruptly stood and crossed the room. Without seeing his face, she sensed his outrage. Fury bombarded every nook and cranny of her room as though there'd been an explosion. She clutched the bulky fabric of her collar and drew it tightly to her throat. When he finally turned to face her, a hardness she'd never noticed before slashed his features. If she didn't know he wasn't a violent man, she'd be terrified by the hard, thin line of his mouth, the hostility in his darkened eyes.

When he spoke, his tone was abnormally level and tight with control. "You don't know me at all, Skye. You don't want to. Are you so afraid of love? Or is it only me you fear loving?"

"I'm not afraid," she insisted on a sharp intake of air.

"Oh, no?"

In two or three long strides, he towered over her, and before she knew what was happening, he'd lifted her from the chair and held her in place against his solid chest. On her astonished groan his mouth took hers in a hard, urgent kiss that tore through all the barriers she'd set between them. Skye was helpless to do anything but give in to the demands of his tongue as it parted her lips. Mac was irresistible, and she was on fire.

When he finished with her and let her go, she stood on wobbly legs. Her lips were swollen and throbbing for more attention. Her heart beat out an irregular pattern inside a body that was so hot, she might have been torched. Mac was right. She was afraid of him. All the more reason to . . .

"Skye?"

Mac's voice, softer than before, as was his demeanor, drew her attention. He stood a foot in front of her. She saw the question in his searching gaze. "I'm attracted to you," she said a bit shakily. "I admit it." She drew herself up. "But that doesn't change a thing."

He exhaled deeply, and roughly combed his fingers through his hair in a confused gesture. "Dammit, woman. I love you and I think you love me. Is money more important than what we feel for each other?" He paused and waited for her answer. None came. "Is it, Skye?" he demanded.

Skye's gaze fell to the floor. A future with Mac wasn't possible. There was nothing to be gained by explaining to him that it wasn't money she wanted. A man with his wanderlust would never understand the value she placed on stability. And respect, a notion Mac undoubtedly knew little about, was important. She couldn't respect a man who thought no more about the future than where today's meal was coming from.

"Some things are more important than love," she finally said, hating the calloused sound of her own words, but not more than the anguish in his gaze when her eyes met his.

"So that's the way it is?" he asked, beaten.

"Yes."

THIRTEEN

"Our stay was delightful." Betty Halpern beamed as she took the receipt from Skye.

"Any luck with your house hunting?"

"Yes, indeed," she answered enthusiastically.

"Then we'll be neighbors soon," Skye speculated. She held out her hand. "Let me be the first to welcome you as residents of Prospect."

"It's premature for that," Earl Halpern insisted.

"That's true, dear," his wife added, and Skye let her unaccepted handshake dangle at her side.

"Which property are you looking at?" Skye asked.

Judging from the stricken expression on the woman's face, either she didn't understand the question or she'd developed a sudden attack of nausea. When response came, it was Earl Halpern who spoke. "Call it superstitious, but until the deal is done, we'd rather not say."

The Halperns finished checking out, the insurance salesman soon after. Ali had left for school a couple of hours earlier, and Mac . . . She didn't have the vaguest notion where he had gone after breakfast.

A faint scent of chocolate drifted into the lobby. Skye inhaled the sweet aroma, which became more pronounced as she made her way to the kitchen. The clock confirmed her suspicion that Ali's three layers of double-chocolate cake were about done.

"What smells so good?" Mac walked in through the back door and sniffed the air.

Skye pulled the pans from the oven and set them on top of the stove to cool. "It's Ali's birthday cake."

"What time do the festivities begin?"

"Her friends will be here at six."

"Anything I can do to help?"

"You've already done enough," she blurted irritably. He stepped behind her, causing her to stiffen in anticipation of some sort of a comeback.

"I promised Ali I'd stay for her party, and I intend to do that," he said to her back, sounding resigned. "I'll leave in the morning."

Eyes wide and unblinking, Skye stood completely still, clutching an oven mitt, her fingers digging into the metallic fabric. "In the morning," she muttered through a tight throat. "Good."

"I didn't like them," Ali said, referring to the Halperns. Her brow narrowed in a disapproving gesture. "I'm glad they're gone, and hope they never come back."

Skye set a stack of paper cups on a tray sitting on the kitchen table. "I sensed you weren't particularly crazy about them," she said, remembering how unusually subdued her sister had become around the couple. "They seemed nice enough to me, and they might move here permanently."

"For real?"

"That's what they said."

"Yuk. I hope not."

"Why are you so against them?"

"That Mrs. Halpern was always asking questions, and I saw her snooping around upstairs."

Skye let out a small chuckle. "She was a bit nosy, huh?" When Ali nodded her agreement, Skye added, "I think she's the curious type, that's all. As for the snooping, I gave her permission to look around."

"You did?"

"Of course. The woman likes antiques and old buildings."

"I don't know." Ali looked skeptical.

Skye scavenged candles from a drawer and set them next to the three-layer cake she'd frosted minutes before. "We've got plenty of time to figure out how we feel about the Halperns," she said playfully. "Right now we'd better concern ourselves with getting ready for your party."

Ali beamed and studied the cake. Her tongue flicked hungrily across her lips, and there was a mischievous glint in her eyes.

"Oh no you don't." Skye swatted at Ali's hand, keeping her from fingering the frosting.

"Just one little taste?" Ali pleaded.

Skye handed her a chocolate-rimmed bowl. "Satisfy yourself with this."

Ali scraped the bowl with her finger while Skye set fourteen pink candles and one white one for luck on the cake and mentally checked off a to-do list. The outside grill was set up, and hamburgers and hot dogs waited on a plate in the refrigerator to be cooked. Accompanying salads were prepared, while unopened bags of potato chips rested in glass bowls on the counter. Paper plates, napkins, cups, and cutlery were stacked on a tray for easy transport to the backyard picnic table.

"We'd better get those balloons blown up and streamers hung," Skye said, noticing the time on the clock.

Ali preceded her to the door, stopping before leaving the kitchen. "He's really going?" she asked, turning to Skye.

"Yes, in the morning."

"I know," Ali said in a subdued tone. "I got it all wrong this time." Sad eyes met Skye's. "Didn't I?"

Skye wrapped her arms around Ali in a loving embrace. "No," she reassured. "Lots of what you said came true."

"Huh?" Ali took a step back and eyed Skye curiously.

"Well," Skye began tentatively, "you said Mac was going to help us, and he's done that. Why, just think of all the repairs he's made around here."

"But I thought he'd really be able to help us," she countered, and Skye knew she referred to her premonition about Mac's supposed money.

"We can't expect others to solve our problems," Skye gently told her. "I think you know that."

Ali nodded her response. "I wish he wouldn't leave, though. I like him. You do, too; I know you do."

Skye couldn't deny it. "Yes, I like him," she admitted, making a sizable effort to sound nonchalant. "But we both knew from the start he wouldn't stay here for long. And who knows?" she added with a cheerfulness she didn't feel. "He may be back this way one day." Skye swatted her sister's behind. "Now, come on. Let's get those decorations up."

Mac had beat them to the chore. They found him out back amidst a rainbow of color. Red, blue, and yellow streamers hung from tree branches and fluttered gaily in the breeze. Bright balloons were strung in bunches and tied to low limbs, the backs of chairs, and even merrily floated from the four corners of the redwood picnic table.

He was centering a vinyl covering on the table when he spotted them. "It's too short," he announced, tugging from an end until the red and white checks met the edge of the table, leaving a gap of several inches on the other side.

Skye stepped to the opposite end of the table, bristling when she accidentally brushed Mac's arm in passing. Facing him, she noticed he looked freshly shaven and had donned a clean plaid shirt and jeans. "I don't have a tablecloth that fits any better," she said, and pulled the colorful vinyl in her direction until both ends were bordered by an equal amount of wood.

Ali surveyed the decorated yard. "This is great," she said, and gave Mac a smile full of gratitude.

Mac patted the top of her head. "Glad you like it."

"Oh, I do. Thanks."

"Yes, thank you." Skye added her own gratitude. "We were running behind schedule, so this was a big help."

"I enjoyed doing it."

Skye turned from his smile, which didn't quite hide a mix of sadness and condemnation. "Why don't you head inside and get changed?" she asked Ali. "I can manage the rest," she assured her, and on a girlish giggle, Ali ran toward the house.

"This was a nice thing to do," she told Mac, her gaze taking in the decorations.

"You sound like you're surprised that I'm capable of doing something nice," he returned, making Skye flinch at the brittle sound of his words.

"Not at all," she snapped back, then immediately searched the path her sister had taken, worried that she'd heard the harshness in her tone. Thankfully, she was already in the house. This was Ali's special day. Skye wouldn't let anything spoil the festive mood. Not when it might be the last good time either of them would know in their home. She banished the unwelcome thought. Milo would come through with the loan, she reassured herself.

Without looking directly at Mac, she sensed his scowl and felt his dark gaze on her. He was picking for a fight, but she wasn't about to give him one, and decided the best thing was to leave the scene before either of them said things they would later regret. But she didn't manage more than a few feet before he cut her off by stepping in front of her.

"Are you ever going to stop running away?" he asked through clenched teeth.

"I won't fight with you," she answered, smothering the urge to do just that.

"I don't want to argue, either."

"Could have fooled me," she couldn't keep from saying, but at the same time, attempted to sidestep him.

His hand on her arm stopped her. "What I want," he said sharply, "is for you to stop running from your feelings for me."

"We've already been through all that," Skye said in exasperation.

"No, we haven't," he returned, his tone heavy with insistence.

Skye's gaze went to his fingers tightening around her arm. "This isn't the time," she told him sternly, and wrenched herself free.

"When is the right time?" he asked her back as she hurried up the porch and through the door.

Never. Mac silently provided the answer she'd refused him. Skye had made her feelings perfectly clear last night. How many times did he have to hear that she didn't want him, didn't love him?

The boys banded together on one side of the picnic table, leaving the girls to sit opposite them. Normal behavior for thirteen- and fourteen-year-olds. Skye smiled at the scrubbed, slightly embarrassed faces of the boys as the girls corralled them into conversation.

Dressed in stretch designer jeans that laced up the ankles, a pair borrowed from a friend, Ali was perched at the end of the table, happiness radiating from her broad smile and sparkling eyes.

The sun was low in the sky, the horizon aglow with warm oranges and golds. A soft breeze carried the faint scent of lilacs in bloom and sounds of bubbling chatter and laughter.

Skye noticed Mac walking toward the grill. He waved to her. "I'll get the fire going."

She nodded, and even when he turned away, she watched his movements, the sureness in his step, the way his hair captured the breeze. Her heart tugged at her chest knowing she'd see him no more after tomorrow.

"Open your presents," one of the girls demanded of Ali, drawing Skye's attention back to the festivities.

"Go ahead," she said when Ali looked to her for approval.

Box after brightly wrapped box was opened with alarming speed, the colorful ribbons and paper scattered quicker than Skye could gather them. "Oohs" and "ahs" followed each unraveling, the loudest and longest praise going to a rhinestone-studded white blouse.

Skye took a small package from her jeans pocket. "This is from me." She handed the little square box to Ali.

"They were Mama's," Skye said with a catch in her throat when Ali eyed the delicate pearl earrings. "I think she would have wanted you to have them."

"Oh, thank you!" Clutching the pearls in her hand, Ali rose and threw her arms around Skye's neck in a big hug. "I can't wait to put them on."

"I'll help you," Skye offered, and took charge of the gold balls Ali tugged from her ears, then helped ease the fourteen-karat posts of the pearls into each pierced ear.

"How do I look?"

"Beautiful."

Ali's friends concurred.

"I've got a little something for you, too," Mac said, stepping up to Ali.

"You do?"

He offered a present the size of a shoe box covered in pink paper. "It's not much," he said as she peeled away the wrapping. "I hope you'll like it, though."

"Oh, Mac!" Ali lifted an oblong oak keepsake case in her hands. "It's beautiful."

"Your initials are on the inside of the lid," he told her, and she opened the box to see. Her fingers traced the carved letters, then flowed over the blue felt lining the bottom.

"Did you make this?" Ali asked.

"Yes."

"I love it."

Skye stepped forward and stood next to Mac. "That was very thoughtful of you," she told him, meaning the praise, and feeling more than a little guilty for some of the less than kind things she'd said to him.

"It's perfect," Ali went on. "Not only did I get these pearls, but now I have a place to keep them. Thanks."

"You bet," he said on a wink, then went off to attend to the grill while Skye went to the kitchen and readied the rest of the meal.

A couple of dozen hamburgers later, everyone seemed satiated. "Hope you all left a little room for cake," Skye said over the loud chatter as she carried the chocolate confection to the table and lit the circle of candles.

"Make a wish," several children commanded in unison when Ali stood over the flicker of lights.

She closed her eyes tight. Skye had an idea about what her sister wished, and hoped it would come true and they would be able to stay in their home. For a second, Skye was tempted to make a wish of her own. If only that's all it took, she agonized, knowing that saving the inn hinged on very real things, very real people. In the end wishful thinking wouldn't make a difference. And no amount of wishful thinking would turn Mac into a responsible, reliable man whom she could trust completely. Still she smiled warmly at Ali, who'd blown out all the candles in one breath.

"That clinches it," Mac said from the other end of the table. "Your wish is bound to come true."

Ali's smile broadened, while Skye's drooped. Ali didn't need encouragement to believe in the impossible, but then, Mac himself believed in the impossible, wanted the unattainable. The way he'd wanted her to acknowledge her feelings for him as though she could ignore the fact that they had no future together was a case in point.

Ali made a long slice through the center of the cake, then turned the knife over to Skye. Mac stepped beside her and handed her one plate after another until everyone was served. She licked frosting from her thumb and lifted her gaze to see him staring at her. She quickly avoided his gaze and the longing she saw in his eyes.

"Allow me." He lifted her hand and slowly sucked the icing from her index finger.

Skye nervously jerked her hand away, but one look around and she was satisfied no one was paying attention to her and Mac. Even so, she didn't want him doing that, not when he made her feel as though she'd stuck her finger in a live socket. Her entire body was still tingling when she spun on her heels and went inside.

Minutes later she heard music coming from the radio she'd taken from the parlor and set in the yard before company arrived. She glanced out the window over the sink. Artificial light staved off the dark of night, and she watched as several of the girls partnered off and danced, all the while trying to coax the boys to their feet. Skye searched the yard for Mac. She didn't see him anywhere.

A bell in the lobby rang.

"Can an old coot get a six-pack?" Rudy asked when Skye entered the hub of the inn. "And maybe a chew?"

"You know better than that." Skye led the way to the store. "Tobacco's not good for you," she said, reenacting the playful scolding she'd given him many times.

"Humph."

"Neither is that much beer," she added when he stacked not one but several six-packs of brew on the counter.

"Ain't all for me," he explained. "The boys and I are havin' a friendly little poker game tonight."

"Oh," Skye said sourly, remembering the times Henry Walker had crawled through the front door at dawn, broke and drunk from what he'd always referred to as a "friendly little game." Of course, his drink of preference was bourbon, and his losses could be counted in the hundreds. Rudy and the boys never played for stakes so high, and at least their alcohol consumption was limited to beer, the very reasons why Henry never partook of their company, calling the local game "child's play."

Mac stuck his head through the door of the store. "Ali's looking for you, Skye." When he saw Rudy, he stepped inside. "I'll take care of this," he offered, and when she looked hesitant to leave, added, "One of her friends is getting ready to leave and wants to thank you and say good night."

"The party must be starting to break up." She checked the time on her watch. "I promised to take some of the kids home."

"You go on now." Rudy waved her out. "Your young man will take care of me."

Mac wasn't her young man, even if the whole town thought so, but correcting Rudy was futile. He'd only assume she was being modest. "If you're sure?" She looked to Mac.

"Go ahead," he insisted, then added as an after-thought, "unless you'd like me to drive Ali's friends home. I'd be happy to do that."

"No, I'd rather do it myself," she answered quickly, and perhaps a bit sharply. Her dependency on Mac was already too great, and she had to stop relying on him.

The toe of Mac's boot caught on something or other, making him stumble, and his right knee crashed into the hard, pebbled edge of the worn and cracked sidewalk.

"Damn," he muttered, not from any pain—he was impervious to that—but because he'd had so much to drink that his senses had abandoned him. He clutched the shiny object at his feet and focused hazy vision on what appeared to be an old, bent bicycle tire rim. He tossed it aside, off the walkway, his muddled mind wondering who'd put the damned thing there for him to fall over in the first place. Was the whole town against him, conspiring to get him to leave? And who had turned off the streetlight? Oh yeah, now he remembered. Prospect didn't have streetlights.

He wobbled to a standing position. All of Prospect wasn't against him. Only Skye. And her mind was made up about him. She'd left him with no doubt about that. She wanted him out of her life since, as far as she knew, he couldn't offer her financial security. He'd been a fool to attempt softening her heart, and wrong to think her feelings for him extended beyond a few nights in bed.

Face it, pal, the lady doesn't love you enough.

"People don't change." He mumbled the jangled thought out loud. How often had he heard that particular saying without believing it? He wasn't so sure anymore.

"Case in point, Mac Morgan, fool of a man."

He'd been in love twice in his life, both times to women who valued money more than him. Was he destined to fall for fortune hunters? Hell, maybe he ought to chuck everything and go be a monk somewhere.

One thing was certain. He should have left town the first time Skye had asked him to leave. That realization and the sour mood that followed were what led him to take Rudy up on his offer to join the poker game.

But he'd found himself paying little attention to the cards in his hand or the conversation around the table. No matter how hard he'd tried, he couldn't seem to focus on anything except Skye's rejection of his love, and beer hadn't drowned his depression or numbed his heart against the pain. And how he had tried. Beer after beer after beer until he'd lost count completely.

Slowly, fighting the dizziness in his head and nausea in his stomach, Mac staggered up the street toward the inn. God, he felt rotten, and couldn't remember the last time he'd been this drunk, but knew it had been a long time ago.

"Damn." How had he allowed himself to get to this state? "Damn."

"What the . . . ?" Skye bolted upright in her bed to the sounds of someone trying to break down the front door. Not that she'd been sleeping. If anything, she'd had little more than fitful catnaps through the night. The clock beside her bed confirmed that dawn was a couple of hours away.

She jumped out of bed, grabbed her robe, and scurried toward the sound. Throwing on the light switch in the lobby, she looked at the front entrance. Sure enough, someone on the other side of the locked door was twisting the handle and pushing at the oak veneer until it shook in its frame. Skye's glance went to the telephone, and she thought about calling the sheriff in Lindsay.

"Damn door." Mac's curse was loud enough that Skye recognized his voice immediately.

She ran to the door and unlocked the bolt before he made more noise and woke Ali. What was he doing out there anyway? She'd assumed he'd turned in early when she arrived home at half past ten and didn't find him downstairs.

She gasped when she saw his face. "Mac?"

He tugged at an imaginary hat, his eyes darting upward as though searching for the invisible cap. "Ma'am." He gave her a stupid smile, a drunk smile, then hiccuped. The muscles in his mouth and jaw sagged out of control.

"You're drunk," Skye charged.

"You betcha," he said, stepping inside, leaning forward precariously.

Skye stepped aside, ducking what she thought was his imminent fall. Somehow he managed to straighten instead. "Do you know what time it is?"

"Time, time, time," he mimicked in singsong fashion. "Give us a little kiss." His red eyes caught hers.

"You smell like a brewery."

"No kiss?" He wobbled some more.

"How did you get this way?"

His eyes rolled and his head bobbed. "Get what way?"

"Drunk!"

"Just played a little poker," he got·out.

"And I bet you lost all your money?"

"Mo . . . ney," he repeated. "Don't have money. No money."

"Wonderful," Skye muttered under her breath. There was nothing to do now but get him to bed. "Let's get you upstairs." Skye slipped his arm across her shoulders, letting some of his weight rest on her. "Steady now," she said, moving him up the stairs.

"That's me, Mac steady rock. No. That's steady as a rock." His foot caught on a step. He was too heavy and slipped out of her hold.

"You're a disgrace," she scolded, but helped him up.

"Ah, come on," he mumbled while they took the rest of the stairs tentatively. "A little kiss."

When his cheek brushed hers, she pushed his face away with her hand. But the action was a defense against her own emotions, not Mac. Even in his current state, he managed to polarize her body into one throbbing mound of desire. Now she knew how her mother must have felt all those times she'd overlooked Henry's drunken arrivals home in the middle of the night. But Skye wasn't her mother. She was stronger than that. For Ali's sake and for her own, she had to be.

They made it to his door, Mac leaning into her while she twisted the knob. Once in the room, she guided him to the bed. He plopped on his back, the springs squeaking from the sudden impact. He managed to partially pull himself up and tried, unsuccessfully, to reach his boots with his hands.

"I'll do that." Skye tugged until the boots dropped to the floor. When she came to the head of the bed, his hand caught her wrist in a hold that was surprisingly strong.

"You'd better get some sleep," she choked out.

"I . . . uh . . . didn't want you to see me this way. Sorry." His apology held a hint of sincerity, even through the slurred speech.

Skye felt her mood soften until she remembered all the times Henry had made the same kind of apologies, and the hurt in her mother's eyes when she finally acknowledged his faults and many betrayals to herself and Skye.

"I'm sure you are," she finally said. "But it won't stop you from behaving like this again and again, just like . . ." Her words trailed. There was no point in saying more.

Mac's eyes glazed over with a sudden hardness. "Go on, finish," he dared.

"No point. Just get some sleep." She began backing out of the room.

"That's it. Run off again." He pulled himself to a

sitting position. "But hear this, Skylar Carson." His words were sharp and astonishingly clear. "I'm not your stepfather. I'm nothing like him or that rotten bum you hooked up with in St. Louis."

Skye shook from his assault and her own anger. "What I know," she snapped, "is that you promised to leave in the morning, and here you are, too drunk to get up anytime in the A.M., and too broke to go anywhere. How convenient. And now you're counting on my sympathy. You know I can't turn you out in your condition."

"I don't count on a thing." His eyes narrowed to slits, and she saw his jaw working. "Don't you worry," he continued in a tone that was softer and harder all at once. "I'll keep my word. You'll be rid of me tomorrow. Guaranteed."

As if he'd exhausted every last ounce of energy, he fell back in the bed and was snoring within seconds. Skye closed the door behind her when she left the room, and stood against it for a long while. She shivered in fear. She wouldn't make him go. How could she when he'd lost his last bit of money? Never mind that the blame for his condition was of his own making. She still couldn't turn him out. Yet how could she not? If she allowed him to stay after tonight, she'd end up doing it again. And again.

FOURTEEN

Skye's bewildered gaze fastened on to the bumper of Milo Craft's black limousine as it made its departure down the street. Only when she couldn't see the car any longer did she look at the sealed envelope the chauffeur had handed her.

"A delivery from Mr. Craft," he'd said, and was off with no more explanation than that.

"What's that about?" Ali skipped down the porch steps and headed for the edge of the street where Skye stood.

"I think Milo has come to a decision," she said, hoping Ali didn't sense the trepidation she was feeling.

Ali pointed to the white envelope in Skye's hand. "Is that it?"

"This?" Skye waved the envelope. "No, no. This is just a note, probably to let me know he's back in town and to set up a time when we can get together."

"Where's Mac?" Ali asked, apparently accepting Skye's explanation. "He didn't come down for breakfast."

Skye relaxed, grateful for the change in subject. She didn't know what was in the envelope, but was determined to open it in private in case the words inside were not the ones she wanted to read.

"Mac is sleeping in this morning."

"Oh," Ali said in such a way that Skye wondered how much she knew about last night's events.

"He came in late. Did you hear him?"

"I heard something. The noise woke me up. When I looked, you were helping him upstairs." Ali hesitated. "He drank a lot, didn't he?"

"Yes."

Ali's head lowered, but not before Skye noticed the disappointment behind her eyes and sensed she was remembering all the times Henry had come home in the same condition. "He's never done that before," she said in his defense after a second or two.

"No, he hasn't," Skye agreed. Ali's school bus came into view. "Have a good day." Skye waved her sister good-bye.

Only after the bus moved off did she go inside to check the contents of the envelope. The note was probably exactly what she'd told Ali, an appointment card, but ripping open the envelope, she couldn't help wondering why Milo hadn't simply called.

She read. No appointment. No real explanation. Only a *no*. The typed message was brief and formal. After consideration of her proposal, Milo Craft regrets he cannot justify investment in so risky a venture.

Skye turned the single sheet of expensive linen in her hand as though she were certain there had to be more. He couldn't say no to her loan without some explanation. And he'd known her family too many years to be so brief, so cold, with his response. At the very least he could have told her face-to-face that he wasn't going to lend her the money!

On an angry impulse she marched to the car and set a course for the Craft Ranch, taking a brief second to glance up at the open second-story corner window. Mac was still sleeping it off. She'd checked on him minutes before, found him snoring loudly. All morning she'd fretted over what she was going to do when he finally did wake, but that worry would wait. At the moment she needed explanations from Milo, her family's old and dear friend.

When she arrived at Milo's door, the maid ushered her in with a friendly smile. Martha had been with the Crafts for two decades and instantly recognized Skye.

"Good to see you, miss. You should come around more."

"Thank you, Martha. It's good to see you, too. I'm here to see Milo."

"He's on the veranda having breakfast. I'm certain he'd like it very much if you joined him."

Skye doubted that but followed Martha. She found Milo alone. He sat at a table sipping coffee and reading a paper.

"Look who's come to visit," Martha said excitedly.

Shock registered in his features before he concealed it behind a controlled smile. "Good morning, my dear." He stood when she neared. "How good to see you."

"I'll bring you some breakfast," Martha offered as Skye took a seat across from Milo.

"No, thank you. I'm not staying."

"That'll be all, Martha," Milo said in a way that made it clear the maid's presence was no longer welcome. Milo picked up a silver coffee urn. "At least you'll have coffee?"

"No. I didn't come for coffee or breakfast," Skye said brusquely.

"I see." He filled his own cup.

"Why, Milo?"

His old gray eyes lifted to hers, his hard, steady gaze meant to intimidate. "If you are referring to your request for a loan, I thought I made that perfectly clear."

"You made nothing clear," Skye said, refusing to avert her eyes.

He forced a smile and patted her hand that rested on the table. "Such animosity. We can't have that. Not between us. Why, your father and I were such good friends."

"Then why won't you lend me the money?" she persisted.

"Do you disallow my right to refuse?"

"No, I don't. But if, as you say, you were my father's friend, at least you could have given me a reason for your answer. All I got," she continued, her tone growing harsher and stronger with conviction, "was a note that said no loan. No reason. And you had it delivered by your chauffeur. Didn't even tell me in person."

"I see I've hurt you." Milo pushed back in his chair. "I apologize. Forgive an old man a momentary lack of courtesy. I've been so busy. There have been so many demands on my time. Nonetheless, you are right, I owed you a personal explanation."

Skye leaned forward, letting her arms rest on the table. "Then perhaps you would like to explain now. Surely you saw the potential in the prospectus I submitted?"

"Perhaps," he admitted. "In the right hands."

"My family has owned Carson Inn and the property around it for three generations. Who better than me to turn it into the thriving business it once was?"

"Ah, but you are so young, my dear. You have no experience. You and Ali would be far better off making a life for yourselves somewhere else." He leaned into her as though offering a secret. "Get away from the old place. Build on new dreams."

"Let me get this straight. You're not saying my plans for the inn are bad, you're saying I am."

"Now, now. Don't take it so personally. After all, you and your sister—"

"Mornin', Milo. What a glorious day." Betty Halpern bounded onto the veranda, her smile and quick gait stalling the moment she spotted Skye. Color drained from her thin cheeks and she looked as if she might faint. "Oh dear," she muttered.

"Mrs. Halpern?" Skye looked from her to Milo, whose mouth was open in bewilderment.

"Oh my." Mrs. Halpern approached Skye cautiously. "You weren't supposed to know, not now anyway."

The Halperns were purchasing property in Prospect. Their secretiveness hadn't made Skye suspicious, but now she knew she should have been. "It's the inn," she said to the distressed woman. "You want my inn."

"You're waiting to buy it cheap when the bank forecloses," she added, putting all the pieces in place. "Then you and your husband will put all my plans into effect."

Mrs. Halpern's guilty gaze dropped to the ground, confirming Skye's speculations. "Why do this to me?" she asked Milo. "How could you?"

"They're family," Milo said evenly. "Betty is my second cousin and they want the place."

"And you don't care how they get it!" Skye slammed her fist against the table, causing him to jerk back in his chair.

"You are not being fair, my dear. I see it as doing you a favor."

Skye wanted to shout and scream and wring Milo's scrawny neck. And she wanted to cry. Even as she cursed him, hot tears threatened her vision. "Damn you," she screamed, and ran from the house before she could say or do things that would only make the situation worse.

She drove home like a madwoman, oblivious to everything but her anger and hurt. Operating on pure instinct, she dashed up the stairs to security and understanding—to Mac.

Was he still sleeping? She knocked loudly on his door. No response.

"Mac." His name came out like a plea as she opened the door and stepped inside.

He wasn't asleep. He wasn't in bed at all. The old four-poster had been stripped of its coverings, the clothes she'd lent him were folded and piled on the mattress, and there was no hint that he'd been there at all. Skye doubled over and groaned against an agony that pained her entire body.

Mac was gone.

More drizzle. Mac let the pencil drop from his hand onto the open file he was supposed to be studying and went to the window, where he eyed the Dallas skyline without really seeing it. Was it his imagination or had it been raining for a month? Well, he was sick of it, and sick of this office and this city and his whole damned existence.

Existing was all he'd been doing: eating, here and there; sleeping, little; and working—or pretending to. When would his torment end?

He'd left Prospect determined not to look back, but

that's all he did. Twenty-four hours a day he relived his time with Skye. Replaying their lovemaking, remembering how soft and warm and right she felt in his arms, was all that kept him from completely caving in to a depression so deep that he feared he was capable of slipping from reality altogether.

"Made a decision about that Crayton deal?" Roger stuck his head through the door.

Mac cleared his throat and squared his tie. "Umm, no. Not yet." He sat at his desk and stared down at the file his assistant had handed him hours before.

"We need to move on this if we're going to put in a bid," Roger reminded him, something he'd never had to do until recently.

"Maybe we shouldn't bid?"

Roger stepped fully into the plush office, careful to close the door behind him. "You're asking me?"

Mac shrugged.

Roger dropped into one of two matching Louis XIV chairs that adorned the space in front of Mac's massive Italian hand-carved desk. "We've known each other a long time," he said. "You're the boss, and heaven knows working for you has earned me quite a piece of change what with the investments I've made on your say-so."

"Is there a point to all this?" Mac asked impatiently.

"I'd like to think our relationship goes beyond that of business associates. I'd like to believe we're friends."

"We are."

"Then as your friend, I'm telling you that you've got to—" Roger gulped "—you've got to do something, otherwise you'll soon be a major has-been with nothing left but memories of grandeur."

"What do you want me to do?" Mac asked raggedly,

his glance going to the desk calendar as he counted off the days since he'd seen Skye.

Roger exhaled deeply. "I don't know." He ran nervous fingers through his thinning hair. "Maybe there's nothing to do. Just tell me you'll pull out of this, whatever it is. If you tell me that, I'll believe you and won't worry."

Pull out of this. Roger wanted the old Mac Morgan back again. Hell, so did Mac. He slumped deeper in the chair and swiveled it around to face the dreary gray sky out his window.

He knew what he had to do.

If Skye wanted his money, then she would have it. And he, God willing, would have her. Please, God, let her stay with him forever.

He stood and faced Roger. With newfound determination and a tone carrying all the authority of the old Mac, he ordered, "Get in touch with the First State Bank of Lindsay." He scribbled information on a paper and handed it to Roger. "Find out about this loan. See if the payments are current. Do it pronto. There's no time to waste."

"If the mortgage isn't current?" Roger wanted to know.

"Then pay whatever amount it takes to keep the property from foreclosure."

"Thank you for calling," Skye said to the man on the other end of the phone. "I'll let you know my decision in a day or two," she reassured him before hanging up.

Who was she kidding? There was no decision to be made. Of course she would take the job as day clerk at the lodge on Lake Eufala, and ought to be feeling lucky for getting the offer, considering the number of applicants who had applied.

She was a fool for not accepting the position immediately, but couldn't bring herself to say the words. To do so meant an end to all hope, no matter how futile, that she'd find a way to save the inn.

Skye bit down on her lower lip. She was always trying to get Ali to face reality, and now she was the one who needed a reality check. There was nothing she could do; the lawyer she'd seen three weeks ago confirmed as much. Nothing but go gracefully, with a smile on her face for Ali's sake, and build a future. She just wished leaving the past behind didn't hurt so much. And she got physically ill every time she thought about the Halperns owning Carson Inn. Would they change the name?

Skye shook her head as if to throw off the question. She had to keep her mind off those things she couldn't change and concentrate on the future. A future without Carson Inn. Without Mac—something else she was helpless to do anything about.

She slapped her open hands against her thighs. "Time to move forward," she said with as much enthusiasm as she could muster, and forced a smile.

There was one good thing amidst the stampede of bad ones. Ali had come to grips with losing the inn, and although there had been a few rough moments, she accepted as fact that they were leaving. At last her sister was living in the real world instead of escaping to a dream one. Too bad it had taken so great a loss to finally bring her around.

"Find your young man yet?"

Skye turned to see Rudy sauntering toward her. She'd been so preoccupied with her own thoughts that the sound of the door opening hadn't registered in her mind.

"No, I haven't," she answered. *And never will*, she added silently. Not that she hadn't tried to track Mac down by asking darn near every person in town if they'd seen him leave, or knew anything about his whereabouts.

She'd never been so miserable as she was after he left, and telling herself that the cause was Milo's betrayal and losing the inn was, at best, a partial truth. It hadn't taken her long to figure out that she could go through anything, suffer any loss, as long as Mac was by her side. Without him she was slowly dying inside.

Skye hadn't forgotten her conviction that he wasn't a man to stick with one job, one place, or even one woman. But she had come to the startling conclusion that a broken heart was best left for later, not sooner. And she had figured out that she couldn't cubbyhole people, presume their behavior matched her expectations of them. Thinking back to her St. Louis days, she'd thought Kyle honest and honorable. She'd thought the same about Milo Craft. Both had betrayed her, their actions totally contrary to her expectations of them.

Mac, on the other hand, might not let her down. There was a chance that he would stay with her always. And she was ready to gamble on him. If in the end she lost, at least she would have had his love for a time.

And so she'd looked for him. Old Mrs. Garver remembered seeing Mac get into a cab the morning he left, and even recalled the name of the cab company. After much cajoling, Skye convinced the dispatcher to confide that Mac had asked to be driven to Lindsay. He was dropped off in the midst of the business district. She'd spent numerous hours making inquiries in the area, but to no avail.

Days later she received a letter in the mail from Mac. Scrambling to rip it open, excited and certain that he would tell her where he'd gone, she had been disappointed instead. There'd been only cash . . . for the room, the one-line note read. No address, no nothing. Only a postmark that identified Dallas. Of all the places. She'd never locate him in a city that size. And maybe he didn't want to be found, not by her anyway.

Why Mac thought he owed her money was a bewilderment, but she didn't question where he got the cash. Gambling, money from an odd job, who knew? And she certainly didn't care how he chose to live. Not any longer. All she cared about was that she loved him and she'd lost him, and all because she had been afraid of becoming like her mother. Well, she wasn't her mother, and Mac wasn't her stepfather. They were altogether different people with their own choices to make and their own chance at love. If only she had realized all that before she pushed him from her life.

"Don't fret, missy." Rudy winked at her. "He'll turn up again. Leastways that's what your sister says."

"She does?"

"Sure 'nough. Was tellin' me yesterday how she expects to see him return most any day now."

So Ali still believed Mac would be a part of their lives. Maybe she even thought he'd ride into town in a long white limo, his pockets brimming with money, and would save the day after all. If she really believed all that—and according to Rudy, Ali did—then Skye was worried. Ali's bravado was no more than a cover-up for what she actually thought.

"You okay, missy?"

"Huh? What?" Skye dragged her attention back to Rudy. "Yes, fine."

"I'm right sorry for all the troubles you been having," he said solemnly. "Maybe that man of yours will come back soon, before you have to leave."

Skye knew Rudy was trying to be helpful and probably thought he was saying something that would make her feel better. But all he'd accomplished was to add to her already shattered heart.

Rudy set a carton of eggs and a loaf of bread on the counter. "Your man sure can put on a drunk," he said, remembering, and fondly from his expression, Mac's last night in Prospect.

Skye immediately came to Mac's defense. "It only happened once," she shot back.

"Well, sure," Rudy agreed quickly.

Skye put the cost of the purchases on his tab and handed him the sack.

"Thanks, missy."

"No problem." Skye waved him off and wondered if the new owners would allow tabs.

She closed the door to the store, went through the lobby, and was halfway up the stairs when once again she heard the familiar squeak of the front door.

"Forget something, Rudy?"

When he didn't answer, she stopped and twirled on her toes. But the man standing just inside the door wasn't Rudy.

Skye grabbed the banister and held on tight. Her gaze locked with Mac's and she shook all over.

"Hello," was all he said, but the sound of his voice rumbled through her like a flash fire.

Seconds had gone by before she realized that he was somehow different. Then she noticed his clothing. He wore an expensively cut slate gray suit. Apparently he'd come into a little cash. That he would spend it on clothing surprised her.

Hands stuffed in his pants pockets, he stood staring

up at her. His mouth twisted into a lopsided grin. "I missed you," he said softly, tentatively.

That's all Skye needed to hear. She leaped down the stairs, taking them two and three at a time. "Oh, Mac!" She ran into his waiting arms. "I missed you, too," she got out before his mouth came down on hers in a hard kiss filled with longing.

When his lips finally left hers, he set her in front of him. "I love you, Skye. I want to marry you."

Skye's heart beat erratically in her chest, and she was so happy, she thought she might burst. "Marry me?" she repeated.

"Before you say no, I have something to tell you."

"I wouldn't say no."

His gaze was full of surprise. "You wouldn't?"

"No, Mac."

"But . . . I . . ." He was dumbfounded.

"You were right," she pronounced. "I was running from you and from my feelings. I was afraid you'd break my heart," she went on. "But I love you, love you with all my heart, and I want to be with you. I just never believed you'd come back and give me another chance. I almost don't believe you're really here now."

"I'm here, all right, and I'll prove it." He pulled her to him and claimed her lips. Mac swelled with love for Skye. It was him she wanted, not his money. He doubted any man had ever loved a woman as much as he loved her at this minute.

"Whew." Skye took a moment to catch her breath. She had to tell him about the inn and her new job. "Ali and I are moving," she told him, not knowing quite where or how to begin. "I have a job at a lodge on Lake Eufala."

"What about Carson Inn?"

"I've lost it," she said, without even trying to hide the pain behind the words. "But it's okay. Now that you're here, I can stand anything."

"I'll never leave you," he promised so sincerely that she believed him.

"The thing is," she continued, "I want you to come with us."

"As your husband?"

"Yes. Oh, yes."

"And you don't care in the least whether or not I contribute financially to the household?" he questioned, thrilled but mystified by her change of heart.

"But you will contribute," she insisted. "I love you, and Ali loves you. You'll return that love. What bigger contribution is there?" She eyed him expectantly. "You will come with us?"

"How can I refuse such an offer?" he said, and smiled down on her.

Skye let out the breath she'd been holding. All was right with the world, or at least had a good chance to be. But when her gaze sought his, the glowing smile that had been there moments before had been replaced with . . . Was it fear? "Mac?"

"I wish I was poor," he mumbled, more to himself than her.

"What are you saying?"

"That I'm rich. Filthy, stinking rich, and I'd give up every penny of my money if it would buy your forgiveness for the charade I played."

Skye looked at him in confusion as she tried to comprehend what he was telling her. "I don't get it. Is this a joke?"

"I wish."

Her chuckle sounded tinny. "Let me get this straight. You have lots of money." Then it hit her. "You mean

you won a bundle gambling. Is that it? Wonderful!''
she rambled on. ''A little cash will help us get reestab-
lished—''

''We're not talking about a few hundred or even
thousands,'' he interrupted. ''I have millions.''

Millions of what? Skye's muddled mind wondered.
Surely he wasn't talking about *dollars*.

''Mmmm.''

''Mmmm?''

''And I didn't get a dime from any poker game or
horse race. I earned the first million a decade ago in
oil; the next came from investments.'' He shrugged.
''Then more oil and more investments and, well, you
get it.''

Skye opened her mouth to speak, but words wouldn't
come. She didn't get it at all. Mac had to be playing
a joke on her, but his serious expression couldn't be
denied. ''This can't be,'' she finally managed, her
words squeaking out.

He reached for her arm and led her to the front window. ''Look.'' He motioned toward the curb.

A stretch limousine, all white and gleaming, hovered
in front of the inn, looking as out of place on the worn
Prospect street as a polar bear in the desert. A chauffeur
stood as if at attention alongside the vehicle while several local citizens stopped to ogle the car.

''Yours?'' Skye asked in disbelief.

''It's a bit flashy.''

''A little,'' she agreed wholeheartedly.

''I thought a show of wealth would impress you into
marrying me,'' he admitted, and Skye began to understand some of what he'd been telling her.

''You are rich,'' she said in wonder. ''And all the
while you were here, you pretended to be a . . .'' She
didn't finish. There was no need.

"Please, Skye," Mac pleaded. "Understand why."

"I'm trying."

"I didn't mean to deceive you."

"You didn't?"

"Think back," he implored. "You assumed I was a drifter."

"That's what you looked like."

He told her about the twister and his failed vacation. "Don't you see, you and Ali seemed to be talking about me when I entered your store, and I thought you were playing a joke on the stranger in town. Then when you assumed I needed a handout, I played along. At the time it seemed innocent enough. I didn't expect to stay."

"Why did you?"

He brought her into the circle of his arms and gently rocked her. "Because of you. I think I must have fallen in love with you the moment I first saw you. But it took me a while to figure that out. Then I was afraid to tell you, didn't know how you'd react. Later I didn't say anything because you turned down my marriage proposal, and idiot that I am, I thought it was because you wouldn't marry a poor man, and I had to know you loved me for myself."

"You thought money was so important to me?" Skye asked, unable to conceal her disappointment.

"Like I said, I'm an idiot."

"No more than me," she admitted, realizing he had cause to think that of her. "But why come back?"

"I discovered that I had to have you, no matter the price." His gaze fell in shame. "I had a foolish notion that I'd buy your love."

Skye backed away. "I don't know what to say."

He narrowed the space between them and set his

hand on her shoulder. "Say you love me. Say you'll marry me."

The front door slammed on its hinges. "There you are." Skye started at the brittle sound of Betty Halpern's voice.

"I don't know how you did it." She wagged an angry finger at Skye while Mac maneuvered himself between the two women. "But you haven't seen the last of me or my husband."

"You're not making sense," Skye snapped. "And the last thing I need is more confusion."

"Where'd you get the money?" Betty asked, but her tone was accusing. "I can imagine what you had to do for it." Her gaze drifted through the window to the limo, then to Mac. She reared back in surprise. "Why, you're that handyman!" she exclaimed, her gaze taking in his expensive apparel.

Mac's mouth twisted into an ironic smile. "Sure am," he told her. "I don't know what your gripe is, lady, and at the moment I don't much care—"

"I have every right to be upset," she interrupted. "My husband and I were counting on buying this inn." Her angry gaze shifted to Skye. "I don't know how you managed to make the back payments," she said indignantly. "But you can just bet there will be another time. You'll be broke again. Then we'll see."

"That's enough." Mac grasped the woman's arm and escorted her out the door, down the front steps.

"My cousin will hear about this," Betty Halpern warned. "Milo Craft won't stand for anyone manhandling his family."

"You tell ol' Milo that Mac Morgan sends his regards." When Betty shot him a puzzled look, he added, "And be sure to tell him that my fiancée, Skylar Carson, and I are looking forward to putting Carson Inn back on a paying basis.''

"Well, I never.''

Mac left Betty on the stoop, mouth agape.

"You heard?'' he asked Skye sheepishly.

"Every word.''

"Tell me I didn't speak out of turn,'' he asked hopefully. "Say you're not angry.''

"You didn't. And I'm not.'' She smiled up at him. "Oh, Mac, you made the bank payments.''

"Then you forgive me? You'll marry me?'' He picked her up off the floor and twirled her around.

"Yes! Yes to both,'' Skye got out between her laughter. "For better or worse. For richer . . . or poorer.''

"Yippee!'' Mac whooped, then set her on the floor. "I love you, Skye.''

"I love you, Mac.'' Her lips met his in a kiss that sealed their love.

This time both Skye and Mac heard someone enter the inn, and turned to see Ali gaping at them.

"Mac!'' She raced into his open arms. "I knew you'd come back. I just knew it.''

"How's my girl?''

"Great. Now.''

Skye stood by, watching her sister's elation over Mac's return. And she wondered if Ali had some special gift to predict the future, after all. The experts said no, insisted that her predictions were the product of an overactive imagination locked in the mind of a creative person, a child who had lost so many people that she wanted an escape from reality. Skye had staunchly believed them. Until now.

"I'd say you were right on with that prediction of yours,'' Skye praised Ali.

"Umm." Ali clasped her hands together and shuffled her feet. "About that."

"What is it?" Skye asked when Ali's cheeks reddened and her gaze lowered.

"You were right the whole time. My prediction about Mac was a dream, that's all."

"What!" Skye's puzzled gaze met Mac's. "I don't understand."

"I went to the library today to look up some information for my paper. You know, Skye, the one for civics class." She didn't wait for a response. "Anyway, there's a magazine. Guess I saw it before, but honest, I didn't remember seeing it, not until today."

"A magazine?" This certainly was a day of many surprises and even more confusion. "What's that got to do with your prediction?" Skye wanted to know.

Mac slapped the side of his head with his palm. "I get it!" he exclaimed.

"I wish I did," Skye said.

"That magazine?" His gaze locked on to Ali's. "I was in it?"

She nodded. "Pictures and everything," she said in a small voice, and motioned in the direction of the limousine. "That, too." She turned to Skye. "I'm sorry."

Suddenly everything was clear. Ali had seen a picture of Mac in a magazine. Later, when losing the inn became a real possibility, a hero, Mac specifically, turned up in her dreams to save the day.

"You don't have to be sorry," Skye told Ali. "You didn't deliberately try to deceive."

"No, but you always told me my dreams weren't real. You were right."

"No, Ali, I was wrong."

"Huh?"

Skye took Mac's hand, then Ali's, and gave them both a squeeze. "We have to live in the real world. I still believe that."

"Yes," Ali interjected. "And that means facing problems and finding solutions," she said in a very grown-up voice.

Mac pinched Ali's cheek playfully and gave her an approving wink. "Good thinking, little one."

But it was Skye who said, "Dreams are important, too. We need to have them, cherish them, and pin our hopes on them." Her gaze met Mac's loving one. "And sometimes, every once in a while, one comes true."

SHARE THE FUN . . .
SHARE YOUR NEW-FOUND TREASURE!!

You don't want to let your new books out of your sight? That's okay. Your friends can get their own. Order below.

No. 155 DREAMS AND WISHES by Karren Radko
Skye needs a miracle and in walks Mac. Be careful what you wish for!

No. 105 SARA'S FAMILY by Ann Justice
Harrison always gets his own way . . . until he meets stubborn Sara.

No. 106 TRAVELIN' MAN by Lois Faye Dyer
Josh needs a temporary bride. The ruse is over, can he let her go?

No. 107 STOLEN KISSES by Sally Falcon
In Jessie's search for Mr. Right, Trevor was definitely a wrong turn!

No. 108 IN YOUR DREAMS by Lynn Bulock
Meg's dreams become reality when Alex reappears in her peaceful life.

No. 109 HONOR'S PROMISE by Sharon Sala
Once Honor gave her word to Trace, there would be no turning back.

No. 110 BEGINNINGS by Laura Phillips
Abby had her future completely mapped out—until Matt showed up.

No. 111 CALIFORNIA MAN by Carole Dean
Quinn had the Midas touch in business but Emily was another story.

No. 112 MAD HATTER by Georgia Helm
Sara returns home and is about to make a deal with the man called Devil!

No. 113 I'LL BE HOME by Judy Christenberry
It's the holidays and Lisa and Ryan exchange the greatest gift of all.

No. 114 IMPOSSIBLE MATCH by Becky Barker
As Tyler falls in love with Chantel, it gets harder to keep his secret.

No. 115 IRON AND LACE by Nadine Miller
Shayna was not about to give an inch where Joshua was concerned!

No. 116 IVORY LIES by Carol Cail
April makes Semi a very unusual proposition and it backfires on them.

No. 117 HOT COPY by Rachel Vincer
Surely Kate was over her teenage crush on superstar Myles Hunter!

No. 118 HOME FIRES by Dixie DuBois
Leara ran from Garreth once, but he vowed she wouldn't this time.

No. 119 A FAMILY AFFAIR by Denise Richards
Eric had never met a woman like Marla . . . but he loves a good chase.

No. 120 HEART WAVES by Gloria Alvarez
Cass was intrigued by Peyton, one of the few who dared stand up to him.

No. 121 ONE TOUGH COOKIE by Carole Dean
Taylor Monroe was the type of man Willy had spent a lifetime avoiding.

No. 122 ANGEL IN DISGUISE by Ann Wiley
Sunny was surprised to encounter the man who still haunted her dreams.

No. 123 LIES AND SHADOWS by Pam Hart
Gabe certainly did not fit Victoria's image of the perfect nanny!

No. 124 NO COMPETITION by Marilyn Campbell
Case owed Joey Thornton a favor and now she came to collect his debt.

No. 125 COMMON GROUND by Jeane Gilbert-Lewis
Blaise was only one of her customers but Les just couldn't forget him.

No. 126 BITS AND PIECES by Merline Lovelace
Jake expected an engineering whiz . . . but he didn't expect Maura!

No. 127 FOREVER JOY by Lacey Dancer
Joy was a riddle and Slater was determined to unravel her mystery.

Meteor Publishing Corporation
Dept. 693, P. O. Box 41820, Philadelphia, PA 19101-9828

Please send the books I've indicated below. Check or money order (U.S. Dollars only)—no cash, stamps or C.O.D.s (PA residents, add 6% sales tax). I am enclosing $2.95 plus 75¢ handling fee for *each* book ordered.

Total Amount Enclosed: $_____.

____ No. 155	____ No. 110	____ No. 116	____ No. 122
____ No. 105	____ No. 111	____ No. 117	____ No. 123
____ No. 106	____ No. 112	____ No. 118	____ No. 124
____ No. 107	____ No. 113	____ No. 119	____ No. 125
____ No. 108	____ No. 114	____ No. 120	____ No. 126
____ No. 109	____ No. 115	____ No. 121	____ No. 127

Please Print:
Name _____
Address _____ Apt. No. _____
City/State _____ Zip _____

Allow four to six weeks for delivery. Quantities limited.